GOD OF THE SUN

KIMBERLY LOTH

Cover design by Deranged Doctors

For Will

My incredible husband

For believing in and supporting me

Always

Thank you

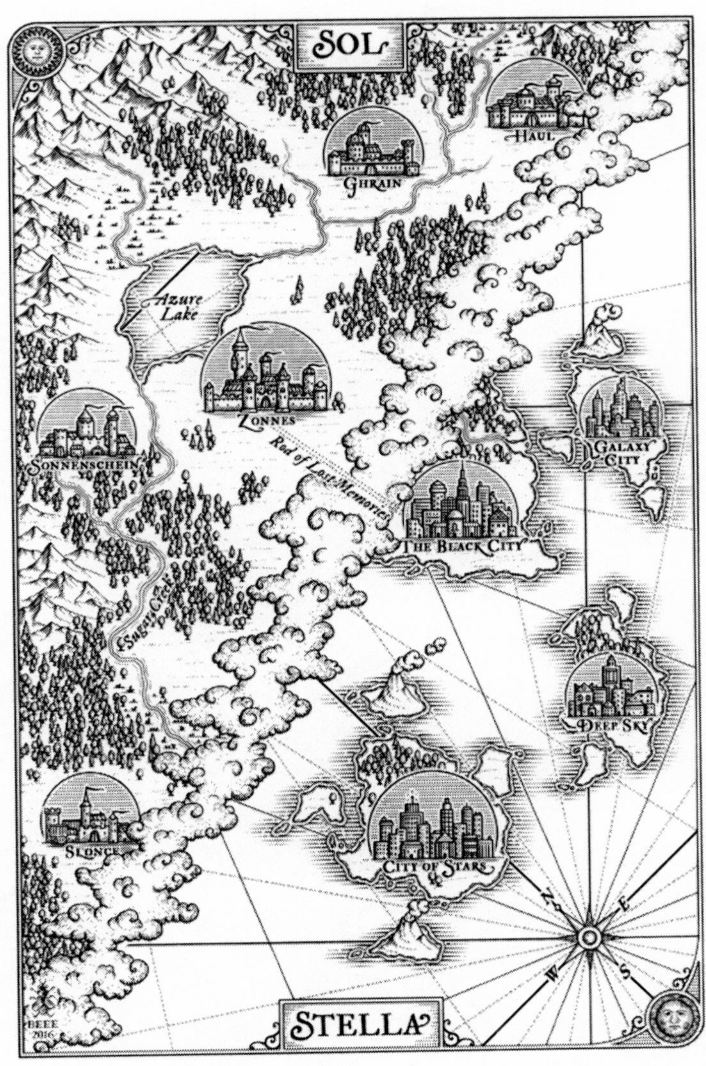
SOL
Haul
Ghrain
Azure Lake
Zonnes
Sonnenschein
Road of Lost Memories
Galaxy City
The Black City
Sugar Creek
Deep Sky
Slonce
City of Stars
N
E
W
S
BEEE 2016
STELLA

Prologue

The Baby

High Prince Leo of Stella sat down at the large circular table. It was rare for them to eat breakfast in the dining hall of the castle, but the rest of his twelve siblings arrived last night at the behest of his sister, Candace, who had an announcement. Of course, he knew what the announcement would be, they all did, but he played dumb anyway. This would be the first grandchild for his father, and so it warranted a special breakfast.

Bright yellow lights hung from the ceiling, and the floor glowed white. Light flowed from nearly every surface, as the darkness could be suffocating. Thank the stars for magic. Leo looked around the noisy table. Over the last few years, the number of people around the table had grown. When they were children, there were only twelve of them, plus his father and his father's wife. Now, couples were starting to emerge. Three of his older siblings were married, and others had steady relationships. At seventeen, Leo had had a relationship or two, but at the moment he was free. Which was a lonely place to be when his favorite sister was about to announce that she was pregnant. Where in the depths were Ari and Sage? They would keep him entertained. But they were always late.

Candace caught his eye, and he smiled at her. She practically glowed. She wore her deep black hair swept up in a twist. He hadn't seen her wear it down since she got married.

He missed having her around. They were the only two siblings who shared the same mother, and that created a special bond between them. But now Candace was a lower queen and had too many responsibilities to come home often.

A hand thumped him on the shoulder, and his eldest brother, Ari, collapsed into the armchair to Leo's right. He sat with his leg flung over the armrest, his blue hair hanging in his eyes. To Leo's left, his sister Sage sat down, flicking her rainbow-colored hair over her shoulder. She had deep purple bloodshot eyes. She yawned and put her head on the table.

"Late night?" Leo asked.

Sage nodded into her arms. "Has she announced that she's been knocked up yet?"

Ari straightened in his chair and poured himself a glass of juice. "She can't be knocked up if she's married."

"She's only been married for a month. My guess is she's a few months along. That's knocked up," Sage said, sitting up and rubbing her forehead. "Remind me to never drink again."

Ari laughed. "You say that every time we go out. The last time I reminded you, you punched me." He turned his attention to Leo. "How come you didn't come out with us last night? I sent you a few messages."

"I turned off my disc. I wanted to spend some time with Candace. She won't be here long."

"Right," said Sage. "You just don't like to party. Maybe you should go live in Sol."

Leo snorted into his glass of orange juice. "If I have to live in Sol, you two are coming with me."

"They'd kick us out so fast. Ugh, what did I do to my hair?" Sage asked, examining the multi-colored locks. She squeezed her eyes shut, and it returned to the brilliant violet she usually rocked. She dug into her pocket, took out a small bottle, and downed it.

Before Leo could ask what it was, Candace stood, and the whole table fell silent, except for Sage, who was giggling. Candace glared at Sage, and Leo squeezed her knee. She covered her mouth and tried to stifle the giggles. The small bottle clinked next to her plate, and he picked it up. The label said "Giggle."

"That's not nice," Leo hissed at her. "Taking this

potion right now. You're going to ruin the announcement." As the tenth child, Sage got away with more than the rest of them, but sometimes she took things too far. This wasn't fair to Candace.

"Sorry." She giggled. "I thought it was Sober. My head is killing me. For what it's worth, the giggling isn't helping."

Candace cleared her throat as the door creaked opened. Every head in the room turned.

An old woman hobbled in. She was large with a pale weather-beaten face, and she wore a bulging tattered coat. An earthy odor emanated from her. She crept slowly to the table and then plucked an apple from a bowl. She took a bite and spit it out, revealing gray teeth.

"Blech, those taste much better in Sol. I need to remember to eat before I come next time." She looked around the table. Her blue eyes pierced Leo's, and he shivered.

The entire table sat in shocked silence. No one moved. Leo had heard the stories about the Old Mother who gave horrible prophecies that required someone to make a great sacrifice. He didn't know anyone who had actually met her. He assumed the rumors were simply scary stories kids told each other.

The old woman cackled and pointed to Candace.

Leo's stomach clenched. Not now. Not her. He pushed his chair back, ready to help Candace if she needed it. He crept around the table and made his way toward her.

"A prophecy I have for you. The vipers grow restless. They long for the blood you deny, and they are changing. If the kingdoms of Stella and Sol are not joined by that child's first birthday, then he will die," said the Old Mother.

She stared at each of them in turn, making eye contact. "And he will not be the last. The union must be strong. You must prove to the earth that Stella and Sol will be forever joined, or the vipers will eat you all."

With a poof and a cloud of dust, she disappeared from their midst. Not a sound was heard in the room except Sage's giggling.

Chapter 1

The Stranger

Screams filled the little house in the middle of the slave village. Zwaantie pushed her white blonde hair out of her eyes and held Mrs. Bakker's hand, making exaggerated breathing motions in the hopes that maybe Mrs. Bakker would copy her and make the birth easier.

Instead, Mrs. Bakker let out another ear-piercing scream and crushed Zwaantie's fingers. Zwaantie's slave, Luna, wiped a white cloth on Mrs. Bakker's forehead. The room was stifling with the wood stove burning. Wilma, the midwife, said it helped the mothers, but Zwaantie thought it just made them hot and irritable. Mrs. Bakker opened her bright blue eyes and stared at Zwaantie.

"I'm sorry, Your Highness," Mrs. Bakker said in between breaths. Zwaantie sighed. She supposed being addressed like that would be the story of her life, as it had for all of her sixteen years, even if she was just trying to do her job.

"Please, call me Zwaantie."

Don't ask for such disrespectful things. No one

should call you anything but Your Highness.

Zwaantie nearly rolled her eyes at the Voice, but then she'd get another reprimand. The Voice was always scolding her and everyone else for silly things they said or did. Thank Sol it could not read thoughts. It was a constant chatter in everyone's heads, reminding them of the rules. Solites learned at a young age to tune out all but the most forceful of the words, or they'd never be able to think.

Zwaantie's mother often reminded her that she should be grateful for the Voice, or else their kingdom would be in chaos all the time. God spoke to them through the Voice so they would always know the right thing to do.

Mrs. Bakker struggled to speak. "Of course, Princess Zwaantie."

Solites believed in hard work, and so even as the crown princess, she was not allowed to sit around and be pampered. If she became queen, she wouldn't be able to perform her midwife duties as often since she'd have to attend to the affairs of the kingdom. She hoped that by some miraculous surprise, she wouldn't have to take the throne, because what Zwaantie wanted most in the world was to be normal.

It was unusual for a member of the royal family to pick such a job since it was so demanding. Her younger brother, Raaf, had chosen to learn how to cook. Her father was a master archer, and Mother was a seamstress. Mother had hesitated when Zwaantie declared she wanted to work with the midwife. But after Zwaantie batted her baby blues, Mother gave in. Zwaantie abhorred royal things, so she chose a job that got her as far from the castle as possible. If Mother had refused, her second choice would have been farming.

For the most part Zwaantie loved her job, except she hated wearing the brown dress. All her dresses covered her body from neck to foot, but the brown dresses always seemed more suffocating. They were tighter in the chest and arms so loose fabric didn't interfere with any medical procedures.

"One more big push. You can do this." Wilma gave Mrs. Bakker a wide toothy smile, but it didn't do any good. Mrs. Bakker bore down, her face twisted in pain. She let out another scream and then collapsed. Zwaantie dropped her hand and rushed to see the baby, her favorite part. She left Luna to attend to Mrs. Bakker.

Wilma sat on a low stool and cleaned out the mouth of the tiny boy with inch wide gold bands tight on his wrists and ankles. Those bands marked him as a slave and would grow with him. Wilma rubbed his back, but he let out no cry, his body a deep purple.

"Quick, grab the bottle of Breathe."

Zwaantie spun around to the wood table and dug into Wilma's leather bag, her chest tightening. The Voice blabbered about the immorality of potions, but she ignored it. In the four years she'd been working with Wilma, she'd never seen a baby or mother die, but they did sometimes. She tossed aside Nopain and Bloodstop and finally found Breathe.

Abomination, the Voice said forcefully. Although the Voice abhorred magic, it wouldn't stop her from using the potions. She tuned out its chattering even though it'd gotten loud, unstopped the bottle, and handed it to Wilma, who tipped the contents into the baby's mouth. As soon as the liquid hit his throat, he sucked in a deep breath and let out a cry.

The knot in Zwaantie's chest loosened. They were out of the woods. She collapsed against the table, relief flooding her body. Wilma wiped the baby down, wrapped him in white cloth, and handed him to his mother, who took him with shaking arms.

As Mrs. Bakker nursed her baby, Wilma observed the girls cleaning up. Zwaantie had become fast friends with Wilma when she started her training. Zwaantie wasn't sure how old Wilma was—probably older than her grandmother, but Wilma had an answer for every question Zwaantie ever asked. She loved that because Mother often used the dreaded phrase: "Because I said so." Plus, Wilma never treated her like a princess, and yelled at both her and Luna equally. Working with Wilma was the only time that Zwaantie felt like a normal person.

Zwaantie was still learning, and she found the work incredibly rewarding. She'd never delivered a baby without Wilma present, but she felt she was ready. She was about to tell Wilma as such, but a knock came from the door. Luna rushed to answer it. The rusty hinges squeaked as she cracked it open.

"Come in," she said, stepping back and opening the door. Luna had a wide smile on her face that told Zwaantie only one person could be on the other side.

Sure enough, Pieter ducked as he stepped into the doorway, his sandy blonde head nearly grazing the ceiling of the tiny home.

"The king has called for you," he said with a nod to Zwaantie.

"Tell him I'm working."

You will go to your father. That is non-negotiable.

Zwaantie sighed. They were always summoning her for dumb things, like what color they should use to decorate the grand hall or what to feed the lower kings and queens. Quite frankly, Zwaantie didn't care. But the Voice would keep talking until she did what he commanded. She thought about arguing, but then she'd have to open her mouth. Zwaantie often spoke aloud to the Voice, but she only did that when no one else was around because she thought it looked weird when people walked down the street talking to themselves. Everyone knew they were arguing with the Voice, but Zwaantie didn't want people to see her doing it.

"Pieter, wait. Luna and I will come. Wilma, will you be okay?"

Wilma gave her a knowing grin. "Yes. I'm going to stay here tonight and make sure there are no other complications. Tell your mother we need more medicine. That was my last bottle of Breathe."

"I will, but I don't think there is a whole lot she can do."

"The mage wagon should've been here weeks ago." Wilma wrung her hands together. They relied on those potions and had no way to produce them on their own, and it wasn't like they could go over to Stella and get them. Potions were the only kind of magic allowed in Sol, though the Voice still discouraged it.

"I'll see if she can have a guard wait by the crossing, intercept a carriage, and send a message that we need medicines." It was the most she could do. Someday she would be queen, and she used to think that meant she'd be able to change things in her kingdom, but the more she learned, the more she realized that there was so much out of her control. She didn't want that job or the responsibility.

Pieter held the door as Zwaantie and Luna walked out into the cool morning. Zwaantie flipped up her hood so that no one would recognize her. Their shoes clip-clopped along the cobblestones, breaking the silence. Tiny houses with thatched roofs lined the road, packed tight next to one another. Slaves went to work as soon as the day broke, so even by mid-morning, there were hardly any people around, save a few guards who watched from the shadows. Pieter stayed close to Luna, and Zwaantie saw them brush hands a few times.

"You know, you are allowed to hold hands," Zwaantie said.

A deep blush formed on Luna's face as Pieter intertwined his fingers with hers. Zwaantie let out a sigh and dropped back a few steps. They were adorable. Luna's caramel skin stood out against Pieter's pale skin, but they seemed to fit so well together. The bands on both of their wrists flashed in the sunlight. All slaves had four bands. One on each wrist and ankle. By the time they were fully grown, the bands were about three inches wide and fit snug against their skin. They never came off.

When they were ten, Zwaantie asked Luna if the

bands hurt. Luna replied that she barely felt them, but she didn't like the way people looked at her because of them. Being a slave was a stigma Zwaantie wouldn't want.

Though, in some ways, she envied Luna. Pieter had been Luna's choice. No one had told her who she had to marry.

Zwaantie had a choice as well, but her pool was smaller. As heir to the throne of Sol, she'd have to marry a lower prince. The problem was she didn't like any of them. There were only four, well five. But the prince from Zonnes didn't count because he was only four years old. Zwaantie was glad he was the only one who lived in the capital city, or she'd have obnoxious princes at her door every day. As it was, she still had to see the other four lower princes once a month. The lower kingdoms of Ghrain, Sonnenschein, Haul, and Slonce were each at least a day's carriage ride from Zonnes, where Zwaantie lived in the high castle.

The princes were yet another reason to not become queen. Every day she found another one, but most centered around the fact that she wasn't a leader. Not by a long shot. She did what others told her. Except for the Voice. She disobeyed it as often as she could get away with because she was so tired of its incessant chattering and never ending lectures, but she didn't think that was a sign of leadership.

Thankfully her mother hadn't brought up the dreaded "m" word yet. Zwaantie had until her brother took his position as Grand Chancellor. Because Mother said that when Raaf returned, she would have to prepare to take the throne. Which, roughly translated, meant getting married. As much as she missed Raaf, she hoped he had to train for a long time.

Four years ago, the grand chancellor had declared that his time was at an end, and Father chose Raaf to replace him. Raaf was only eleven at the time, but Zwaantie knew he was glad to get the position. Next to the king and queen, the grand chancellor held the most power. He spoke to the Voice on behalf of the people and controlled the guards.

She should've told her mother and father she didn't want to be queen when they chose Raaf to be grand chancellor. Maybe if she'd spoken up then, Raaf would be preparing to become king instead.

Who knew how long it took to train the grand chancellor. At least ten years. Maybe even longer. Was anyone ever ready to face God?

A hooded man pushed past Zwaantie and grabbed Luna's wrist. Pieter shoved him away, and Zwaantie rushed to her side.

"How dare you touch my slave." Zwaantie

glowered at the man. She caught sight of his dark face and took a step back. He was from Stella.

"You don't belong here," the man growled at Luna. "Certainly not with those slave bands. Come with me. I will bring you home."

Zwaantie stepped in between them. "Let her go."

The man shoved her, and she nearly lost her balance. "This is none of your business."

Zwaantie stalked to him and lowered her hood. Two guards came running as she knew they would when they recognized her. She hated being reminded that without her royal title she was nothing. She couldn't even protect her friends without using her status. She was pathetic.

"Is there a problem, Your Highness?" one guard asked, glaring at the man. The other guard pushed the man against the wall of the nearest house. "Filthy Stellan, what are you doing in our land?"

Zwaantie needed to play this carefully. She didn't like the way the man talked to Luna, but this was the first Stellan she'd seen in weeks, and they needed medicine. Curse the stars. She should've stayed hooded. She could've talked to the man without having him fear her. Now she was steps away from getting him arrested. She never thought before she acted.

"No, no problem. I apologize if I alarmed you,"

Zwaantie said.

The guard released the man, and he shook out his arms, his black eyes trained on the guards.

"I could have you arrested," Zwaantie said. "But I won't. We are nearly out of medicine. Please return to your kingdom and let the traders know we will pay handsomely for any they bring."

The man narrowed his eyes at her. "What's in it for me?"

Zwaantie bristled. Stellans never did anything unless they got something in return. Everything about them was barbaric and uncultured. That was what happened when there was no Voice. If this man had been a Solite, he'd have jumped to help Zwaantie.

"One month of merchant food." Stellans never took anything for payment except food.

"Two."

Zwaantie rolled her eyes. "Fine, two. Hurry, please."

She addressed the guards in full princess mode. "Would you please make sure this man is given two months' worth of merchant food and is escorted to the border?"

"Of course, Your Highness."

Zwaantie waited until the man was out of sight before they continued on their walk. She let out a breath and replaced her hood. She'd think twice before she showed her face next time. Crime was rare in Sol, and Zwaantie had never had to use guards before.

Pieter held tightly to Luna's hand. The words the man spoke bothered Zwaantie. Luna had been with her for so long that she often forgot Luna didn't belong in Sol. She was from Stella.

"You don't want to go back, do you?" Zwaantie asked, scared that maybe her best friend and slave was unhappy here.

Luna gave her a smile. "No, of course not. I barely remember Stella."

"How could he have gotten you through the wall anyway? The Voice wouldn't let you go," Pieter said.

Solites were forbidden to cross the border, and once Luna's mother signed the slave contract, Luna became a Solite, at the age of four.

"I don't know. It doesn't matter. This is my home. I have no desire to return to the dark." She clung to Pieter and looped her other arm through Zwaantie's. "Besides, I wouldn't have you two there."

As they exited the tiny village, the castle came into view, winking in the sunlight. Its spires reached high into the sky. It was the grandest building in Sol. A smaller castle sat off to the side for the lower king and queen of Zonnes. A handful of fields with an occasional farmhouse separated the slave village from the castle. Merchant homes were on the other side of the castle.

They strolled along the road in the middle of the fields, watching the animals graze. Zwaantie loved the farms, in spite of the smell. They were the lifeblood of their kingdom. Maybe in another life, she could've been a farmer's wife. She'd like that. It was simple and rewarding.

Just before Zwaantie entered the door of the castle, she closed her eyes and turned her face to the sun, letting it warm her face. Thank Sol she'd been born here, where it never got dark, instead of Stella, where the sun never shone.

Chapter 2

The Unexpected Return

They hiked up the long winding stairs to the king's chambers. Pieter pushed the door open, but there was no one there. Luna's mother, Ariel, came running down the hall, her shoes clattering on the floor.

Ariel stopped short in front of them, breathing hard, and she put her hand on the hard stone surface of the wall to balance herself. "What took you so long? Everyone has already gone outside."

"Why?" Zwaantie asked, confused.

Ariel clapped her hands together. "Your brother is returning. Come, they should be here soon."

Luna's face broke out into a wide smile, but Zwaantie's stomach fell. Her brother was coming home. His training was over, and that could only mean one thing for Zwaantie. Marriage.

They followed Ariel down the long hall. Zwaantie dawdled on purpose. She wasn't ready for this. She paid close attention to the portraits that hung on the walls. Normally she raced by them, but today she noticed how the children always smiled but the kings and queens did not. They bore the weight of the kingdom on their shoulders. The last portrait was of her grandparents and her father as a child. Zwaantie had never seen him smile like that. She barely knew him. Mother spent time with her and Raaf, but Father always was too busy. She didn't want to do that to her own children. Ariel held the door open and waved to Zwaantie.

"Quickly, child, they'll be here soon."

Luna and Pieter stood directly behind Ariel, waiting for Zwaantie. She sighed, gathered her skirt so as not to catch it on the door, and stepped out into the sunlight.

She blinked against the bright light. Her eyes adjusted, and she stared out over fields and villages in the distance. Soon this would all be hers.

Zwaantie's mother and father stood near the top of the outer stairs, holding hands. Zwaantie was a spitting image of her mother, with the same blue-green eyes, long blonde hair, and heart-shaped face. Father was tall and broad, with graying hair and a perpetual scowl. Zwaantie took her place next to her mother. Their slaves stood a few steps behind them. Mother nodded to Zwaantie, a small smile playing on her lips. Zwaantie supposed she was excited as her only son was coming home. A son she hadn't seen in four years.

Zwaantie bounced on her toes, the nerves finally getting to her. She hadn't seen her brother in so long. Would they still be friends? His letters had gotten sparse in the last year or so.

"Would you be still? You're acting like a child." Mother gave Zwaantie a disapproving glare. Zwaantie stilled. Otherwise, the Voice would tell her off, but she was having trouble not fidgeting.

Zwaantie didn't understand how Mother could be so calm. They hadn't seen Raaf in four years. He'd sent letters of course, but beyond that, she'd had no contact with him. She missed him like crazy. He was her best friend. Had he changed much, or was he still her Raaf?

Her dread at his return dissipated a bit. Raaf was coming home. She couldn't wait to hear about his training, and she could tell him about her work with Wilma. Plus, she had to fill him in on all the princesses. If she had to get married, then so did he. She wanted him to marry Princess Cornelia from Haul. She was loads better than Princess Luus here in Zonnes.

The sound of horses clip-clopping on the drive came just before the carriage rounded the corner. Four white horses pulled the bright yellow carriage, and Zwaantie squealed.

Hush. Behave like a princess.

Zwaantie sobered. Stupid Voice. She had to listen to it. She had no choice, but it was a real killjoy sometimes.

Okay, all the time.

Zwaantie folded her hands in front of her like she was trained and stood with her head tall and an impassive expression on her face. But the Voice couldn't stop the racing of her heart. Luna brushed at something on Zwaantie's shoulder and smoothed her hair. Zwaantie figured she was having trouble staying still as well.

The carriage came to a stop, and Zwaantie had to restrain herself from running down and ripping the door open. She waited impatiently for the footslave to open the door.

Raaf came out first. He'd grown about a foot, and he'd cut his hair. He used to wear it long, because Mother loved the rich red color. But now it sat just below his ears. His face was stony, which was unusual. When they were kids, the smile never left his face.

"Mother, may I go greet him?"

Mother nodded. Zwaantie took slow steps so not to appear too eager, but she was sure the huge grin on her face would give her away. Luna kept herself so close that if Zwaantie were to misstep, Luna would bump into her.

Raaf moved away from the carriage.

Zwaantie beamed at him. "Welcome back."

"Thank you. Have you been well?" His voice had dropped at least three octaves. He no longer sounded like her Raaf. She bounced in front of him, itching to give him a hug, but knowing that would be inappropriate.

"I've missed you. We need to catch up tonight. I want to hear about your training." She spoke louder than normal and way too fast. But she couldn't help herself. Raaf was home.

He frowned. "I can't tell you anything. I'm sorry."

Another figure emerged from the carriage, and Luna lost her composure.

"Phoenix," she squealed and threw herself at him, nearly knocking her brother over. They were from Stella and much more affectionate. Zwaantie didn't even hug her own mother and was sure the Voice was chastising them, but they didn't seem all that bothered. Phoenix held her tight, and Zwaantie studied him.

When they were children, the four of them were inseparable. They played in the woods on the castle grounds together as if they were all siblings. The only difference was the bright gold bands Phoenix and Luna had on their wrists and ankles that marked them as slaves. That and their deep caramel-colored skin.

Zwaantie never realized what that meant until she was older. There were hundreds of slaves in the castle. Almost all of them were pale Solites. Stellans were rare in Sol, and most were traders who hurried back to Stella the first chance they got. As far as Zwaantie knew, Luna and her family were the only Stellan slaves in Sol.

The year Zwaantie turned twelve, Raaf went off to train in some secret location in the middle of the mountains, and Phoenix went as his personal slave. It was natural for Luna to become Zwaantie's slave. She and Luna were like sisters, and she was sure Raaf and Phoenix had a similar relationship even though Phoenix was a few years older. Zwaantie didn't see how they couldn't, being trapped in the middle of nowhere with no company except stuffy old chancellors and a few guards.

Unlike Raaf, Phoenix had a huge grin on his face that would charm the stockings off most girls.

He'd changed as well. His black hair had grown and fell in loose curls to his shoulders. His face was no longer pointy and sharp, but had matured into a strong jaw.

He let go of Luna and bowed to Zwaantie, and she couldn't help but notice his wide shoulders and the muscles that moved under his gray linen shirt.

His dark eyes sparkled. "Princess, it is good to see you."

Zwaantie's chest tingled as she appraised him. She was expecting children to return, but instead they became men. Extremely good looking, in Phoenix's case.

Phoenix had always been exotic, but she'd never thought of him much different from her brother. She had no business thinking of him now. He was Luna's brother and a slave.

But with his deep piercing eyes, full lips, and caramel colored skin, he was stunning.

Luna beamed at him. "I can't believe you came back. Just in time too."

His eyes danced as he looked down at her. "Just in time for what?"

She pouted and swatted him. "You got my letters. Don't play dumb."

"Well, my baby sister isn't getting married until I approve, and I have less than twenty-four hours to give you my blessing. Where is this Pieter you've been going on about?"

"Standing behind the king. You'll have to wait until tonight to talk to him, but I'm sure you'll love him."

Phoenix glanced at Mother and Father. "He's awfully tall."

"So?" Luna asked with a frown.

"Nothing. Just an observation."

Raaf still hadn't said much. Zwaantie looked at him cautiously. She was jealous of the easiness of Luna and Phoenix. Even if she and Raaf had never been affectionate, they had been extremely close, but now Raaf seemed uncomfortable. Slaves bustled about hauling trunks off the carriage. The horses snorted and stomped their feet.

"Would you like to have tea in my rooms and catch up?" Zwaantie asked him.

He shook his head. "No, we have work to do. Tomorrow I become grand chancellor. Come, Phoenix."

Phoenix gave Luna a sad smile and followed Raaf up the stairs. Raaf stopped for just moment and greeted Mother and Father, but then he swept into the castle.

Luna looped her arm through Zwaantie's and laid her head on Zwaantie's shoulder. "I can't believe they're back. I'm so happy."

Zwaantie kept her eyes on Mother and Father. They had their faces close together and appeared to be discussing something in earnest, but were smiling.

A sinking feeling fell in Zwaantie's stomach. She wasn't happy. Not at all. Raaf was no longer himself.

This was what happened when people grew up. Mother would start asking when Zwaantie was ready to take her crown. One that she could only take on in marriage.

Mother glanced up and glared at them, and Luna moved away from Zwaantie.

"Sorry," Luna whispered. She shouldn't have had her head on Zwaantie's shoulder.

Mother spun around and clomped into the castle. Zwaantie waited until she was out of sight. There was nothing wrong with Luna having her head on Zwaantie's shoulder, but Mother thought it was inappropriate. She wondered how long it would be before the Voice would start yelling at them for that too. It seemed like anytime Mother thought something was wrong, the Voice suddenly did as well.

"It's okay. Let's go inside and see what we can find to do with ourselves," Zwaantie said.

Chapter 3

The Grand Chancellor

Zwaantie was having trouble mustering up excitement. Two of her favorite people were hitting huge milestones, and she should be thrilled for them. In some ways she was. But in other ways, she felt like they were moving on without her. Plus, they were both getting what they wanted. Zwaantie never would. Because what she wanted was to not be royal.

She woke up late, which was normal. Her curtains were still shut, blocking out the bright light. She'd given Luna the morning off. Usually by the time she got out of bed, Luna had her room tidied and a bath drawn.

She sat up and stretched. Zwaantie liked her room, decorated like the summer sky. Her quilt was bright yellow, and her bed had sky blue hangings. Soft green rugs adorned her floor.

She slipped on her morning shoes and padded her way across to her closet where she fingered the dresses, trying to find one she could put on herself. They were all styled the same. Solid colors with long, flowing sleeves. Sometimes they were shaped to fit the body, but they mostly felt like giant tents. The loose dresses were easier to put on than the fitted ones, especially with the slip and petticoat underneath. The fitted dresses had far too many strings for Zwaantie to do them on her own. She wasn't used to doing this by herself, but she wasn't about to let Luna work on her wedding day. The door flung open, and Luna burst in, breathing heavily.

"I'm so sorry, Your Highness. I know what a big day this is for you."

Zwaantie put her hands on her hips and frowned. "I told you not to come. It's your wedding day."

That is not your place to tell her.

Luna gave her a sad smile and closed the door. "Sit down. I'll find your dress. I know you told me not to come in, but the Voice forbids it. We don't get days off."

"But you're getting married. The Voice needs to get a life."

Watch your words.

Zwaantie rolled her eyes.

And your actions.

The Voice was obnoxious. Always bossing her around. And everyone else too, but she was only annoyed when it bossed her. And her slave. It wasn't fair to Luna. She should be able to relax and prepare for her own wedding.

Zwaantie sat and watched Luna flip through the rainbow of dresses. "Find one that will match your colors at your wedding."

"You're still coming?" Luna furrowed her brow.

"I wouldn't miss it. You're my best friend." Plus, this was the one opportunity she had to grant her best friend a gift. If it were up to her, Luna would live in the castle with Zwaantie, like a princess, but like she was so rudely reminded, the Voice wouldn't allow slaves to live like that. But anytime a member of the royal family attended a wedding, a gift was given. The bride and groom could ask for anything under the royal member's jurisdiction. Kings and queens rarely attended weddings because the risk of the couple asking for something too big was there. But princes and princesses didn't have as much to lose.

"What about Raaf?" Luna asked.

"His ceremony should be long over by this afternoon. I'll make sure Phoenix can come too. I'd try for Ariel, but you know how my mother is. She'll never let her go. Now what color will best match your wedding?"

"You mean, the gray I'm wearing?"

Zwaantie scowled. She'd told Luna to pick out one of her old dresses weeks ago.

"You're not getting married in gray." Luna was

pretty good at following Zwaantie's instructions. She had to be. If not, the Voice would give her a thorough telling off.

Luna lowered her eyes. "I tried, Your Highness. I did. But every time I went to put on one to see how it would look, the Voice intervened."

"What did it say? Don't steal the princess's dresses? It must have heard me tell you to take it."

"No, it didn't say anything about stealing. It told me that I was not allowed to wear anything but gray. Colors are above me."

Zwaantie clenched her fists. When she was queen, she'd have words with Raaf about what was and what wasn't allowed. Especially with the slaves. A day off now and then and the ability to choose their own clothes should be allowed. After Raaf became grand chancellor, he would be the only one who could influence the Voice. Though Zwaantie had no idea if the Voice would listen to him or not.

"Fine. But you will take my ribbons for your hair and pick a few flowers out of the queen's garden. That's an order. You tell the Voice you'll be disobeying me if you don't."

You cannot tell her to disobey the Voice. Ribbons and flowers are fine, though.

Luna gave a small smile and nodded. "Thank you, Your Highness."

Luna pulled out a purple dress. "This will look striking at the ceremony this morning."

"I think you're right. Purple is very royal, isn't it?"

Luna helped Zwaantie into the dress, did up the laces in the back, and then brushed out Zwaantie's long blonde hair.

"Are you nervous?" Zwaantie asked. She couldn't imagine what it was like to be getting married, though soon she'd be marrying too. There was absolutely no one she wanted to marry. Her mind strayed to the way Phoenix's face lit up when he saw Luna. She could handle waking up to a smile like that. He was a slave though, and marriage to him would be forbidden.

"A little. But mostly I'm happy. Pieter is going to make a good husband."

Zwaantie shuddered. "Seventeen seems too young to get married."

Luna tugged at Zwaantie's hair and gave her a grin in the mirror. "I'm only a year older than you. Careful, I'll bet the queen will be looking for your husband soon."

Zwaantie shook her head violently, and her braid went flying. "I told Mother that I wasn't ready last month when she tried to sit me next to one of the lower princes at dinner." Now that Raaf was home, Mother would be even more insufferable. Zwaantie was too young. She had to find a way to stall her mother.

"Your mother was married at fifteen. She probably thinks you're long overdue."

"She was deeply in love." Zwaantie hoped her mother would let her marry for love. Mother had been a merchant's daughter. Father was the high prince and fell in love with her on sight. The problem was that she wasn't ready to start the search now.

"I hope so. For your sake. Love is pretty amazing." Luna's eyes got that dreamy look she had every time she talked about Pieter. Zwaantie wanted that. She wouldn't settle for anything less, and she certainly didn't want to think about it for at least another two years. Maybe even longer. Mother and Father could still rule for a few years. Surely she didn't literally mean as soon as Raaf returned. Maybe she could talk her mother into letting her wait.

Luna fixed the braid, and Zwaantie spun around. "Okay, you've done your duties with me today. You don't need to do anything else. Go home and get ready for your wedding. I'll see you just after noon."

Luna nodded. "You don't have to come. Really."

"Of course I do. You're my best friend."

Luna gripped her hands. "Thank you."

Luna slipped on her shoes and clip-clopped out the door. Another slave appeared in Zwaantie's doorway only seconds later.

"You're needed in the great hall, Your Highness."

Zwaantie hurried out of the room. Her steps were loud, but then so were all the rest of those bustling about. Zwaantie saw people from all the lower kingdoms. The lower prince of Haul chatted with Princess Luus. Good, maybe he'd marry her, and he'd be off the table. She glanced around for Princess Cornelia to reintroduce her to Raaf, but couldn't find her.

Apparently, a new chancellor was a big deal. Though, Zwaantie thought, this was dumb. Everyone knew the Grand Chancellor had no real power. He was a face; that was all. Someone who let people think they actually had a choice. Someone to advocate for them with the Voice. But the Voice did whatever it wanted anyway.

The Voice did more than just scold. For small indiscretions, it would shame, and for larger ones, it would create physical pain. Most times the pain went away on its own. Bad things still happened on occasion because the Voice had no warning that the person was going to steal or lie. They would confess to their local chancellor when the pain got bad enough, and he gave their name to the grand chancellor, who would plead for the poor soul's sanity with the Voice. Sometimes the Voice listened, and sometimes it did not. Zwaantie had never done anything bad enough to have to confess. Which was good because now she'd have to confess to her brother. She didn't want him knowing the things she'd done. Though she had thought about doing bad things from time to time.

Zwaantie entered the grand hall from the back of the room. Sunlight streamed through the glass on the ceiling. Large white banners with the symbol of the sun hung from rafters. Zwaantie wove her way through the throng of people to the front. Most didn't even notice her, thank the stars. Because if they did, she'd have to make awkward conversation and submit to their fake bows and suck ups.

She climbed the stairs to the thrones. Mother and Father were already seated. She gave a quick curtsey to both and then took her seat in the smaller throne next to Mother.

"There are a lot of people," Zwaantie said.

"A new grand chancellor is an exciting time. We're so proud of your brother. He's really stepping into his role. You could learn a thing or two from him."

Zwaantie rolled her eyes.

Stop that.

Now that Raaf was back, Zwaantie would have to endure the constant comparisons. She was quite aware that her parents wished Raaf had been born first. Then he could be king. Which meant she would've been free to do what she wanted since chancellors were all men. Her life would've been easier. There would've been no expectations.

"Yes, Raaf will do an excellent job. Where is he anyway?" He'd barely said a word to her since he arrived home yesterday. He was at dinner, but spent most of the time talking to Mother and Father about boring politics.

"A few last-minute ceremonies. What they do out here is simply for show. The real act of passing on the chancellor's staff is done in private."

"Well, maybe the Old Mother will come and spice things up."

Mother gasped, and Father shook his head at her.

Do not speak of such things.

Zwaantie gave them a cheeky grin. She made the same comment every time there was a ceremony of sorts. The Old Mother was a legend who everyone feared. Zwaantie had never met her or even met someone who had, but the legend was that she would show up at grand events and make a terrifying prophecy that could only be avoided if someone made a great sacrifice. Luna told her they had the Old Mother legends in Stella as well. Zwaantie supposed that was why she was so fascinated with the stories. They crossed the borders.

A hand came down on her shoulder. “Nice color, Zwaantie.”

Zwaantie smiled at her brother. He was handsome with his own purple robes. His face had relaxed. Maybe he had just been nervous about today and would turn back into her Raaf after this.

She looked to Phoenix and gave him a small smile. He returned it, and her heart fluttered. She let out a breath. His smile was going to be the end of her. She focused on Raaf.

“You ready?” she asked.

He nodded. “I hope so. This is just a formality.”

He moved past her, his stony face back, bowed to his parents, and took his seat. Phoenix stood behind him. Pieter stepped through a door and stood behind her father.

“What’s Pieter doing here?” she hissed to her mother.

“He’s your father’s slave. Why wouldn’t he be here?” Mother cocked her head at Zwaantie like she couldn’t understand why Zwaantie would even think such a thing. Zwaantie often sent Luna home early or gave her breaks during the day, but Mother never did the same for Ariel. She had that poor woman working from the time the gray skies cleared until thirty minutes before everyone had to be locked in their rooms.

"He's getting married today. He should have the day off."

Mother shook her head. "Your father will release him after the ceremony."

Zwaantie frowned. "And then he'll be back for dinner, right?"

"Of course. All the lower kings are here. Your father needs help dressing for dinner, and he needs a slave to attend to him during the meal."

Zwaantie had meant the question sarcastically. She couldn't believe her father expected Pieter to come back. She supposed if he had many personal slaves like the lower kings and queens, it wouldn't be an issue, but Mother and Father always thought that was too extravagant.

"Can't someone else attend to him tonight? Maybe Phoenix."

"Phoenix will be busy with your brother. Don't be silly. They're slaves, dear. They understand. This is their life."

Normally Zwaantie didn't have issues with the slave system. It was set up so people didn't starve, and for the most part, the slaves were treated well, but times like this she didn't understand why they couldn't even give them a small break. The system was implemented a few hundred years before.

Zwaantie didn't know how it even started.

Her father stood, and the room hushed. With his broad shoulders and brilliant red robes, no one could mistake him for anyone other than the king. Zwaantie always admired the way he led the people. He was beloved. She would not be. She didn't know how to be a good queen.

He held his arms wide and gave the crowd a smile he reserved for his kingdom. Every eye in the room was on him. Zwaantie stared into the crowd. Every color imaginable was represented. Clothes in Sol only came in solid colors. Royalty chose whatever they wanted. Nobility wore every color but purple. Merchants were not allowed to wear red. Peasants wore only yellow and blue. Slaves wore gray.

"Welcome to Zonnes on this glorious occasion," Father said. "It isn't often we get to see the chancellor staff passed on. The last time was when I was but a child. I'm more than pleased to see this honor bestowed upon my son. Thanks be to Sol."

"Thanks be to Sol," Zwaantie and the rest of the crowd repeated.

Father took his seat and the current grand chancellor stepped in front of them. He wore bright white robes and carried a large golden staff.

"Sol has been good to us and the Voice benevolent."

Mother nudged her. She'd zoned out, and now Raaf held the staff, and they were all standing. Stars. What had she missed?

She brought her hands together to clap for him with the rest of the crowd. Most people had smiles on their faces, and she supposed she should be happy for him too, but this was just one more thing that would take him away from her.

Chapter 4

The Wedding

Zwaantie hated mingling. She never said the right thing, and she hated talking about the affairs of the kingdom. Just once she'd like one of the princes to ask if she'd read his favorite story or ask about the babies she delivered.

She was much happier just hanging out with Luna. Plus, at things like this, she always felt like people were just talking to her because she was the future queen. She never voiced her thoughts out loud. That would be rude.

She glanced at the glass ceiling. The sun was nearly at high noon. She searched the crowd and found Father. Pieter still hovered behind him.

"Father," she asked, interrupting his conversation with the lower king of Sonnenschein.

You shouldn't interrupt.

"Yes, dear?" He gave her his full attention. That meant he didn't like the conversation he was currently in, because this was rare.

"Pieter is getting married at noon. Don't you think you should let him go?"

Impertinent girl. Do not talk to your father that way. A small pain flashed across her head.

Father pursed his lips and cocked his head. Then he raised his eyebrows. “Uh, yes. I forgot. Pieter, you may go. Be in my rooms by five to help me dress.”

Pieter bowed to Father. “Yes, Your Majesty.”

Behind Father’s head, Pieter mouthed “Thank you” to Zwaantie and disappeared. One boy rescued. Now she had to rescue another. She’d be lucky to get to the wedding on time. She found Raaf deep in conversation with the previous chancellor. Zwaantie tapped him on the shoulder, the earlier chastisement for interrupting still stinging.

He turned to her and gave a forced smile. “Hello, dear sister. What can I do for you?”

The old chancellor leaned on his walking stick. His face was wrinkled, and his eyes sunk so far back that they nearly disappeared. No wonder he was ready to give it up. She hoped the position wouldn’t be as hard on Raaf.

“I’m going to Luna’s wedding.”

“Thank you for letting me know. I’ll see you at dinner.”

Zwaantie frowned. “I think you should come with me.”

He glanced down at her. “Why? It’s a slave wedding. I’ve got better things to do.” This was not like him at all. What was going on?

"Because she was your friend too."

Raaf sighed. "She was my playmate when we were children. Honestly, Mother should've known better than that."

Zwaantie clenched her fists. She wasn't going to win this one. "Well, I'll take Phoenix with me then. He'll be back in time to help you dress for dinner."

Raaf glared at her. "No, you won't. I need Phoenix."

Zwaantie's voice rose a couple of notches. "Why the dark would you do that? He's her brother. He needs to attend her wedding." She stomped her foot. This was ridiculous.

Calm down.

She seethed. Now the Voice wouldn't even let her be angry.

"Careful with your speech, Zwaantie. Someone might think you grew up on the streets of Stella. I need my slave. He's not coming with you. You better go if you want to get there on time."

"Fishbrain," Zwaantie muttered under breath.

That was not appropriate. A small pain flashed across her forehead, but it was worth it.

Raaf grabbed her arm. "You will not use that foul Stellan language in my presence again. I am the grand chancellor, and you will treat me as such."

Zwaantie ripped her arm out of his grip. "I thought you were my brother."

His eyes flickered, and for a second, she saw remorse. Good. Maybe he needed to be reminded.

She stomped away and didn't breathe again until she hit the hallway. She squeezed her eyes shut for a second. What was wrong with Raaf? He was not the same person who went off to train. She couldn't think about that right now because she had a wedding to attend and couldn't be late.

She raced to her room and grabbed her green cloak. Merchants wore green cloaks, so she wouldn't stand out. She didn't want to ruin Luna's wedding by turning the attention on herself. Having the crown princess at a slave wedding would make everyone forget who was getting married.

The air outside was getting cooler. Fall was on its way. Zwaantie loved the leaves changing color and the nicer temperatures. Plus, the mage wagons came over from Stella. That was her favorite thing. They came twice a year and brought new potions, but they also always had fun magic, things that weren't technically allowed in Sol; yet, they somehow got away with.

She made her way through the fields to the slave village. The chapel stood in the middle of the little neighborhood. Zwaantie had never been in this one before.

She stepped inside and was surprised to hear the sound of laughter. Though the royal chapel was brighter, it was always a quiet, peaceful place—laughter was forbidden. Plus, slaves were normally somber and quiet. Luna wasn't when she was around Zwaantie, but that was only when they were alone. Everyone in the pews was engaged in conversations with those around them. The atmosphere was happy, in spite of the dull gray color that permeated the room. From the clothes they wore to the bare rough stone walls.

Zwaantie looked to the tinted window in the ceiling, and stared at the sun. Windows were perched over the top of the chapel, so no matter what time of day, you could find the sun. You could generally tell what time it was by what window the sun was in. It was high noon, so the sun was in the north window.

"Sol be with me," she muttered and closed her eyes, as was custom when one looked at the sun.

Zwaantie took her place in the back of the chapel and sat, her hood on. She already stood out as everyone else was wearing gray, but no one said anything to her.

The sounds in the chapel died, and Zwaantie turned. Pieter and Luna stood at the back holding hands, a ribbon tied around their wrists. It was a brilliant blue and was striking against the gold bands. Zwaantie rose, and as Luna passed her, she smiled.

The minister stood in front of the tiny crowd and turned his face to the sun.

He recited the wedding sermon, and Zwaantie watched Pieter and Luna. Pieter had only been at the castle for a year, but he and Luna had eyes for each other from the moment he showed up. She and Luna had many giggles in the evening when Luna would tell stories of her courtship. Zwaantie wasn't surprised a month ago when Luna declared she was getting married. Zwaantie had hoped Luna wouldn't rush things, but such was the way in Sol. When her mother decided that Zwaantie should get married, her own courtship would be only be three or four months.

The ceremony was short, and at the end, Pieter kissed Luna. Zwaantie felt a small pang of jealousy. No man had ever looked at her that way. Would she ever find love like that?

Zwaantie followed the crowd out of the chapel and waited behind others to congratulate the couple. She lowered her hood, revealing herself. Immediately everyone dropped to the ground and pressed their faces to the dirty street. Zwaantie grabbed both Pieter and Luna before they could bow as well. She hadn't wanted to reveal herself, but if a royal gift was to be given, it had to be public.

"Stay," she said to Luna and Pieter.

Luna took a deep breath and made no move, so Zwaantie let her go. Pieter nodded as well.

The rest of the crowd was still prostrate on the ground. She wouldn't be able to convince them to stand. No matter how much she pleaded. The Voice was stronger than her command.

"As is custom, when a member of the royal family attends a wedding, you are allowed to ask for a royal gift. What do you wish from me?"

Luna opened her mouth and closed it again. "It is possible…" She frowned. Then she squeezed Pieter's hand. "Your choice."

He cocked his head for a moment. "We'd like our own home so we don't have to share with my family."

"It is done. I'll speak with the housing master when I return to the castle. Now, I must go and let you attend to your festivities. Congratulations."

Zwaantie was troubled. Luna was about to ask for something, but didn't. Zwaantie wanted to know what that was and why she didn't ask for it.

Chapter 5

The Boy

Zwaantie was almost to the palace's back door when she ran right into Phoenix. He bowed deeply, his black curls falling into his face. Zwaantie had the sudden desire to brush them away.

"Forgive me, Your Highness. I wasn't looking where I was going."

Zwaantie waited for him to come out of the bow and meet her gaze. His eyes were beautiful. "It's okay. Where are you going in such a hurry?"

"I was hoping to make it to the wedding. If you're heading back, I'm guessing it's over."

"It is. I'm sorry. But if you hurry, you can probably catch some of the after party." She didn't stay because no one would relax around her. It wouldn't be fair to Pieter and Luna. She imagined their parties were much more fun than the royal ones. Stars, she hated being a princess.

He creased his thick eyebrows. "What after party?"

"All weddings have parties, right?"

"Not slave weddings. We don't have time. There is

a reason it was held during the noon hour. A lot of slaves get lunch then. Most of them are probably back to work by now."

Zwaantie wasn't sure what to think of that revelation. "Well, since you couldn't attend the wedding, would you like to go for a walk with me?" Zwaantie was missing her youth. Her brother was now the grand chancellor, and her best friend was married. Phoenix was the only one left who had no other responsibilities, other than serve her brother. Soon he would be the only one.

He hesitated for a moment. Then a tentative smile spread across his lips. "Sure."

They followed the path to the queen's garden. The flowers smelled heavenly. Birds played in the fountains, and butterflies fluttered around her head.

"I'm sorry you had to miss your sister's wedding."

He shrugged. "I knew it was a possibility. I'll congratulate her tonight after dinner."

"How did you get away from Raaf?" Raff'd been such a turd about letting him go, and now here he was.

"He said he had things to discuss with the old chancellor in private, so I left. That happened a lot when he was training. I hung out with the guards quite a bit. As long as I'm in time to help him dress for dinner, he won't miss me."

Phoenix smiled at her, and Zwaantie was again struck by the fact that he was no longer a boy. Working out with the guards must've been how his muscles developed. He looked at her, his dark eyes sparkling, and her heart skipped a beat. She dropped her eyes, embarrassed at her thoughts.

"Now that Luna's married, will you be next?" she asked, hoping for a reason to deflect her feelings.

He laughed. "Oh, no. Not even close."

"Why not?"

"Because I'm not ready for that."

She could completely relate. They came to a fork in the path. One route led deeper into the garden and the other to the woods. "Do you ever miss the times when we were kids, running around in the woods?"

He gave a small laugh. "You and Raaf would get in such trouble when you came back covered in dirt and grass."

Zwaantie chuckled. "And somehow you and Luna didn't."

"Our mother didn't care."

Zwaantie played with the petals on a pink rose. "I miss it. I miss being kids. I don't like how everyone is growing up."

Phoenix shoved his hands into his pockets. "I know. Raaf and I were close until we left for his training. He doesn't even talk to me anymore."

"Me either."

Zwaantie's heart swelled with the unfairness of it all. Life was moving too fast. She looked out past the flowers and saw the pond they used to play by.

"Let's be kids again," she said.

"What do you mean?"

"Meet me by the rock after dinner. Let's play tag in the woods. Just one last time."

Phoenix frowned. "Zwaantie, we're not kids anymore."

She took a couple of steps closer to him. He held his breath, and his eyes bore deep into hers. She wondered what kind of effect she was having on him. "I know. But we can pretend. Just for one night. Please?"

He let out his breath. "As long as Raaf lets me go at a reasonable hour."

She squealed. "Oh, this is going to be so much fun. It almost makes dinner with the lower kings and queens bearable."

Phoenix shook his head. "Not quite."

He left her in the garden a few minutes later, and she wandered by a fountain, deep in thought.

Earlier today, her mother made sure she talked to at least two of the lower princes. Zwaantie cringed at the idea of even considering a life with them. Phoenix though, just the thought of spending time with him made her giddy. That was probably because she was just excited to play again. Though her thoughts were not on how they used to play, but about how he looked at her so seriously.

She shook away the thought of his beautiful face. He was a slave. She made her way to the castle and found the housing office.

The squat housing master greeted her. "How can I help you, Your Highness?"

"I granted a gift at a slave wedding this afternoon. Luna and Pieter would like their own house. Can you make that happen?"

"Of course."

"Thank you. Please outfit it with the best furniture, the kind you would use in the castle, and fill the cupboards with the finest dishes and linens. Also, fill the pantry and icebox with food. Can you do that before this evening?"

The housemaster looked skeptical, but he gave a tight smile. "Of course, Your Highness." Zwaantie knew that was short timing, but she'd seen her mother ask for more, and they always pulled through.

"Thank you. You can deliver the key to my room during dinner."

Zwaantie didn't know what Luna really wanted to ask her for, but she'd make sure her gift was the best she could give.

Zwaantie had several hours before dinner, so she slipped out the side door and down the rocky path to Wilma's cottage. She didn't bother knocking. By now this was practically Zwaantie's second home.

She found Wilma in the tiny kitchen washing herbs in a large ceramic pot. She marched into the kitchen, and Wilma turned.

"I thought I heard you. Did you ask your mother about the medicines?"

Zwaantie leaned on the counter and inhaled the scent of basil and lavender. Wilma's house always smelled amazing.

"No, but I met a Stellan and paid him two months of merchant food to send someone as soon as possible."

Wilma dropped the lavender into the water. "Two months? That seems steep."

"We need the medicine. I'm hoping that by overpaying he'll be honest about it."

Stellans couldn't produce food because they had no sun, so they traded their magic for food. It worked well and provided Sol medicine and other things that made life easier.

Zwaantie didn't want to lose the sun, but she often wondered what it was like on the other side of the wall. Most Solites wouldn't even dream of wanting to see Stella. Almost all the stories of the Stellans painted them as barbarians, but Zwaantie had Phoenix and Luna, so she was more curious than horrified.

"How was the ceremony?" Wilma asked.

"Raaf or Luna?"

Wilma shook out the lavender, sending water everywhere. "Both."

"I enjoyed the wedding more. Raaf seems different." Zwaantie fiddled with a spoon.

Wilma brought her bowl of herbs to the table. "How do you mean?"

"I don't know. He's barely said anything to me. I was looking forward to having my brother again."

Wilma handed her several stems of basil. "Pull the leaves off these and put them in the bowl."

Wilma preached that the best medicine for the mind was work. Zwaantie should've known that if she came here whining, Wilma would put her to work. She did as she was told though because if she stayed long enough, Wilma's advice would be worth it.

"I've known both of you since you were babies. Raaf's always looked up to you. When he left, you were children. Do you remember how he cried?"

Zwaantie did. It was the only time she'd seen him do so. He could barely say goodbye to her. She'd been bawling too, but that wasn't so unusual for her at the time. She was better at controlling her emotions now.

"That's what I don't get. Shouldn't he be more excited to see me?"

"You're not kids anymore. He knows you're about to become queen. When that happens, he'll have to answer to you. That's not easy for someone who was once your best friend."

Zwaantie accidentally shredded a few leaves. Wilma growled at her and handed her another stem. "Try not to ruin these. I don't have an unlimited supply."

"Sorry. I still want him to be my best friend, but he seems so distant."

"Have you talked to him in private or only while your parents are around?"

"Only when Mother and Father are there."

"Try getting him alone. I bet you'll be surprised by how much he missed you too."

"Maybe." Zwaantie wanted Wilma to be right, but she wasn't sure. Raaf felt so far away. She wasn't comfortable with all this change. Adulthood was being forced on her, and she wasn't ready.

Chapter 6

The Cow: Part 1

Luna returned before Zwaantie had to get ready for dinner. Zwaantie protested, but Luna reminded her that Pieter was working anyway, so there was no reason for her not to attend to Zwaantie. On the way to dinner, Mother caught up with them in the hallway.

"Tonight you will be seated next to the prince of Sonnenschein."

Zwaantie groaned.

Stop that. She's your mother. You will listen to her.

"Yes, Mother." Zwaantie wrung her hands. "Is this necessary? I'm not ready to think of marriage. Especially not with Vache. He's horrible."

Mother sighed, but her eyes softened. "I know. Like it or not, the time has come. I know it's scary, but this is just the beginning. Your brother is grand chancellor. It's time for you to start exploring your options. Sonnenschein is a good city and the largest outside of ours. They know what it takes to run a large kingdom. He's smart, and he'd be a good match for you. Be charming."

Zwaantie rolled her eyes.

Stop being disrespectful.

"Yes, Mother." It was easy for her to suggest him. She wouldn't have to look at him every day. He looked like a cow. She and Luna followed Mother to the dining room.

Several tables had been set up in the room in a u-shape so that all could see the king and queen. People sat on the outer edges and slaves served from the other side. Zwaantie took her place next to the cow-man, and he smiled at her. Vache had huge green eyes, wide nostrils, and a fuzzy white patch on his cheek. He was maybe a year or two older than her.

"Crown Princess Zwaantie, it's a pleasure to sit with you." His voice was surprisingly high for a young man his size. Zwaantie had forgotten how annoying it was.

This was going to be a long night. He and his father always made their view of her intelligence clear when they attended the monthly meetings. Vache wanted to be high king and didn't give a piggy's teat about her. Of the four possibilities, he was on the bottom of the list, but the most eager to make a match.

The prince tugged at his collar and adjusted the vest that strained against his girth. They must eat a lot more in Sonnenschein than those in the capital city. Zwaantie had to admit, though, the best cakes and cookies come from Sonnenschein.

Vache spoke again, startling her once more with the high pitch. "You have a lovely home."

"Thank you," she replied, irritated. He'd been to her home dozens of times. Surely he could come up with a better conversation starter.

A serving slave stood before her. "Wine or water?"

"Wine, please." There was no way she would get through the evening tonight on water. The wine was weak, but it relaxed her all the same.

Vache cleared his throat. And then began talking. He talked for the next two hours. Even when his mouth was full, he was jabbering on about something. Watching cattle graze was more exciting than listening to him. There was no way in the dark sky she would marry this prince.

Zwaantie looked around the room so she wouldn't fall asleep. Raaf was seated several people away, and Princess Cornelia was next to him, thank the stars. They looked like they were having a better conversation than she and her wretched prince. Mother and Father sat at the head where everyone could see them. Behind Father, Pieter stood tall, his eyes locked on Luna. Zwaantie didn't know what it would be like to feel that way about someone. To love them so much that you couldn't take your eyes off of them. Slave or not, Zwaantie was jealous of Luna's life.

Vache reached for his goblet and brushed Zwaantie's arm. She jerked away. She needed to stop this right now even if it meant getting into trouble. Then Mother would see that she was too immature to entertain suitors and become queen. This man was a cow, and Zwaantie intended to prove it.

She sat tall, pursed her lips, and with a perfectly straight face said, "Moo for me."

A giggle escaped Luna.

"Excuse me?" Vache scowled. Zwaantie didn't even flinch, just repeated her request.

"I would like you to moo for me. You know, like a cow. Moo." The Voice was going berserk in her head.

Stop being disrespectful.

Apologize to him.

Stop this.

Vache's eyes went wide, and for a half second, Zwaantie thought he'd actually do it. But she was to be disappointed.

"No. I will not be disrespected like this." His chin jiggled.

Apologize.

A pain shot through her forehead. She didn't have the energy to fight it. Everything about tonight made her tired.

"You are right. I don't know what is wrong with me. The wine must've gone to my head. Forgive me."

Zwaantie pushed her chair out and escaped toward her room. She had stayed long enough that her departure didn't draw any unnecessary attention. Luna followed.

Zwaantie flung herself down on her couch and covered her eyes with her arm. She'd screwed up this time.

"Your mother is going to have your tail for that one," Luna said.

"I know. Worth it." Zwaantie gave a grin that she didn't mean, but she couldn't let Luna see her pain. Raaf was grand chancellor. Luna was married. Mother wanted her to take the crown. She would have to be responsible for the entire kingdom. The thought made her physically ill.

Luna sighed and folded down Zwaantie's bed. "If you say so."

A knock sounded on the door. Mother was fast. Zwaantie wasn't ready to face her, but Luna answered it.

"A delivery for the crown princess," Luna declared, shutting the door.

Luna brought her a small box wrapped with a deep green ribbon. Zwaantie opened it carefully.

Then she grinned. "This isn't for me. It's for you."

"What is it?"

Zwaantie handed her the box. Luna opened it and pulled out a key with the number fifty-four etched on it.

"It's your new home. I hope you like it."

Luna clutched at the key. "Thank you. You've been too kind to us."

Zwaantie waved her hand. "Nonsense. You're my best friend. I should've done more." Zwaantie hesitated for minute. She wasn't sure if she should ask or not, because she suspected there was more that Luna wanted. "Can I ask you a question though?"

"Sure." Luna was still staring at the key.

"You were about to ask me for something different at the wedding. What was it?"

Luna shook her head and placed the key back in the small box. Then she tucked the box into the pocket of her faded gray skirt.

Zwaantie sat up straight. "Tell me. I won't be mad, I promise."

"It's nothing, really. The house was so generous."

Zwaantie grabbed Luna's hands and met her dark eyes. "Tell me. Please"

Luna let out a breath. "I was going to ask if our children could be born free."

Zwaantie's heart stilled. Then she did something

she'd rarely done before. She stood and pulled Luna into a tight hug. "I'm sorry. I can't do that. I wish I could."

Luna nodded into her shoulder. "I know. That's why I didn't ask."

The bondage bands were magical. Once placed upon a slave, it was a hundred-year sentence for the slave and all of his or her posterity. Luna's mother was the first, and so there would be at least two or three generations before the bands would fall off. Zwaantie couldn't change that.

Luna pulled away and wiped at the tears on her face. "Come on. Let's get you dressed for bed."

Another knock sounded just as Zwaantie opened her mouth to argue.

Three guesses who was at the door. Mother. Mother. Mother.

Luna opened the door wide. Mother stalked into the room, her thin lips in a tight line.

"You asked him to moo for you?" She raised her eyebrows. "Honestly, Zwaantie. Could you have been any more disrespectful? Didn't the Voice tell you to keep your mouth shut?"

Mother sat in a dainty white chair. She seemed perfect for the chair, her grace and poise filled but did not overwhelm it. She was the ideal queen, something Zwaantie realized she would never be.

She hated the proper stuff.

Zwaantie sank onto the couch. "I don't want to marry. I can rule without a husband."

"But what about heirs?"

Was Mother really going there? Fine. Zwaantie was ready to end this once and for all.

"Raaf can have them. I'm sure he'd be thrilled with the idea that his kids will one day rule all of Sol. I'm not ready to discuss this. Besides, do you think that I can honestly love that man?"

Do not speak to your mother in such a manner.

"Honor is more important than love." Mother spoke with so much conviction. Like it wasn't even possible to consider the other side of things.

Zwaantie was so sick of that argument. If it wasn't about marriage, it was something else. Honor was more important than friends. Honor was more important than self. Honor was more important than pride. Now it was more important than love. Fine. She'd do the honorable thing and become queen, but she was going to control some aspect of her life. She couldn't just give her entire self away.

"I don't see how I can be a dishonorable queen if I don't marry."

"It's your duty to the people of Sol to present them a queen who will give them an heir. Besides, the people expect you to have a husband."

"Love, Mother, I want love." And freedom, but she couldn't express that out loud. She was just as trapped as Luna, if not more.

"You can marry for love. Is there a merchant's son you would rather have?"

"I thought you wanted me to marry a prince."

"I do. But I don't want to see you unhappy."

Couldn't she see that Zwaantie simply wasn't ready to think about that? But…since Mother brought it up.

"You are saying I could marry whomever I like?" Zwaantie couldn't help her thoughts. Phoenix filled her mind. She'd be queen a thousand times over if Mother would just let her control this one small aspect of her life. She wasn't expecting Mother to be reasonable about this though.

Mother sighed and brushed a hand through her hair. "Yes, of course. We are not opposed to marriage outside the royal ranks. We just thought you'd be happier with someone of your own kind. Now who do you want to marry?"

"Suppose I wanted to marry a slave. Then what?"

Stop being ridiculous.

Sometimes Zwaantie hated having two mothers.

"That's impossible." Mother dismissed the idea with a wave. She was right of course. Zwaantie just wanted to hear her say it. "Now you are being silly."

Mother stood and crossed her arms. "It's time for you to grow up. You will be queen, and I recommend finding a husband who will be a good king, like the prince you just insulted."

Zwaantie resisted the urge to stick her tongue out like a child.

"Also, I'm entertaining the lower queens and princesses in my rooms late this evening. Your presence is required. You will give the queen of Sonnenschein an apology."

"Yes, Mother."

Mother left without saying anything more.

"I want to be alone," said Zwaantie. If she was going to go play in the woods, she needed to get rid of Luna.

"But what about your mother? You'll need me to attend to you."

"I'll be fine."

Luna left quickly. It was her wedding night. Zwaantie hoped Father let Pieter off early as well.

Zwaantie had no intentions of going to the see the queens and princesses. She had two hours until midnight, and she had every intention of making the most of it. She'd pay for it tomorrow, but tonight, she was going to be a child. Responsibilities were for those who actually wanted to be queen.

Chapter 7

The Pond

Zwaantie shut her door with a click and looked around. The dark hallway was empty. She snuck down the hall and turned a corner. A slave with arms full of tablecloths scurried by but didn't look up. Soon she was at the back door. She creaked it open and slid out into the garden.

It's late. Go back to your room.

"Oh, you shush," she told the Voice. "I'm not doing anything wrong, just going for a walk. I'll be in before midnight." She could never figure out how the Voice could sometimes scold her for things that weren't wrong at all. There was never pain associated with it, just words, but it was still annoying.

The smell of the flowers overwhelmed her. She loved early fall. Except for the rain. The ground was always squishy and wet. She kept to the stone path where her wooden shoes clacked against the ground. She thought about taking them off because of the noise, but no one was around. Plus, she didn't want to get her socks wet. Not that she planned on staying dry this evening. Every adventure in the woods ended with someone being soaked from the wet ground or an accidental trip into the pond. A smile crept upon her lips without warning. She felt a little rebellious sneaking out to play with Phoenix.

The path wove farther and farther into the garden. She came to a fork and took the left one. The right path would lead to the queen's garden, which was filled with peonies and mums and usually people. The left path led to a pond that smelled like dead fish. Though Zwaantie didn't like the smell, that was where they played as children because no one else was around.

When she arrived, Phoenix was already there, sitting upon a large rock, watching the sun slipping toward the gray. His back was to her, and she paused to watch him. His dark hair settled just above his shoulders. A small thrill buzzed in her stomach. What would it feel like to run her fingers through those curls or have him stare at her with those deep brown eyes?

She squished her way across the grass to him. He heard her and turned. He smiled wide and patted the rock. Zwaantie's dress pulled at her neck as she climbed up. She hiked up her skirt so the dress wouldn't strangle her. She envied the people of Sonnenschein just a little because their clothes allowed a bit of the neck to show. Here in Zonnes, they covered the entire neck. Most of the time it didn't bother Zwaantie, but when she climbed rocks or trees, her clothes tried to kill her.

"You ready to play?" she asked.

"In a minute. I like watching the sky from this rock. When we were kids, I sat out here all the time, even when you three weren't around."

"Why?"

"It's peaceful."

She settled next to him and put her hand on the rock so her fingers barely touched his. He didn't react, but she shivered. She was playing with fire. But she hadn't done anything wrong yet, so the Voice couldn't say anything.

"Where do you suppose the sun goes?" he asked. After midnight, the sun disappeared into the clouds and a deep gray settled across the sky, but it never went completely dark.

"I've no idea. I've always wondered what the stars look like."

"They're amazing. I miss them," he said.

"You remember? Tell me about them."

"Millions of tiny dots in the dark, dark sky. They make me feel like anything is possible."

"Maybe someday you'll see them again."

"Yeah, right," he said, pointing to his bands.

Zwaantie let out a deep breath. She didn't want to

be reminded of his place. She wanted him to be her equal. "Tell me a story. A funny one."

"Since when did you become so demanding?" he asked with a wide grin.

"Because I miss laughing. Everyone has been altogether too serious today."

"Sorry, I'm out of funny stories," he said with a grin.

"You're telling me my brother didn't do one stupid thing today?"

"Nothing worth telling a story over. However, I heard his sister got herself into some trouble." He winked and chuckled.

Zwaantie sat up straight. "How did you know about that?"

"We were with your mother when that oaf of a prince came lumbering over. Did you really ask him to moo for you?" Phoenix raised a brow at her.

Zwaantie let out a bellow, and Phoenix laughed.

"Okay, no funny stories if that's all you've got." Zwaantie hopped off the rock and challenged him. "If you can catch me, you can do whatever you want with me." This was a game the four of them played a lot as kids. The one caught would often be tickled or have their socks stripped off and have to step into the pond.

He crossed his arms and smirked. "Anything?"

Zwaantie nodded and took a half step away from the rock. She kicked off her shoes and pulled off her socks. The grass was soft and squishy.

Put your shoes on. Your feet will get dirty.

Zwaantie ignored the Voice and felt a dull ache behind her eyes. It was bearable. Phoenix eyed her bare ankles and grinned.

"Even throw you into the stinky pond?"

He wouldn't do that. It was a joke they played a lot as kids, but no one ever actually threw anyone into the filthy pond. "Yep, even that."

"You're on." He stood, and she ran. He hit the ground a few paces away from her. She raced toward the woods. He was better in the trees than Zwaantie, but she wanted him to catch her. Though, she didn't want to go into the pond.

The ground in the woods was soft and warm, coated with damp leaves. Zwaantie darted around a couple of trees and then noticed she couldn't hear him. He must've taken his shoes off.

She snuck around a wide old oak tree. Phoenix was nowhere in sight. She dashed out and ran across a small clearing. Something crashed into her from the side, and she went flying. Zwaantie hit the ground on her hip and rolled, but he pinned her down.

"Gotcha," Phoenix whispered into her ear. She

giggled as he picked her up and threw her over his shoulder. She liked the feel of his arms wrapped around her legs. The Voice sighed, but didn't say anything. Technically, they'd done nothing wrong, so it couldn't find anything to lecture her on.

"Where are you going?" Zwaantie asked.

"Back to the pond."

"You're not really going to throw me in there, are you?" A tiny bit of fear crept into her stomach.

"You said anything." He laughed, and the motion shook his whole body. Zwaantie struggled against his arms, but he held tight. He wouldn't throw her into the pond. Would he?

She smelled the pond before she saw it. She couldn't see much from his back.

"Ready?" he asked.

"No."

He laughed and swung her off his shoulder. He laid her on the ground and straddled her, holding both of her wrists in one of his hands. The wet earth seeped into her back, but she barely noticed. His strong grip on her hands, the way his legs felt on her sides, the pressure of his body on her stomach, warmth flooded her body, and her heart raced.

His chest rose and fell in rapid breaths, and he gave her a devastating grin. She wanted to kiss that smile right off his mouth, wanted to run her hands up his chest and embrace him.

Phoenix leaned down so that his mouth was inches from Zwaantie's ear. "You didn't really think I'd throw you in there, did you?"

She shook her head, not daring to speak in case she accidentally said the things she was thinking. She loved the feeling of him pressed against her.

His breath was light on her ear. "But I am going to tickle you until you pee your pants."

Zwaantie squirmed and squealed. His hand found her ribs, and she couldn't help but laugh. He proceeded to torture her for the next few minutes.

"Stop. Please." She could barely get her words out through her laughter.

Then he released her and rolled to the side. Zwaantie propped her head up and faced him. Her hair fell across her hand and into the grass. Luna would kill her tomorrow; Zwaantie's hair would be in thick knots. The blonde would probably be streaked with green from the grass.

Zwaantie reached across and placed her hand on one of Phoenix's. This was a risky move. She didn't even know what she was doing, but she had to do something to appease the desire in her chest.

"We should go. Midnight will be here soon." Phoenix stood. His rejection stung.

"I don't want to. We could just stay here."

Zwaantie sat up and searched his eyes for any indication that he agreed with her. She saw the conflict in his face.

"You know the punishment for being caught out of bed after midnight."

That depended on Raaf's mood. And he wouldn't behead Zwaantie or Phoenix, which was the normal punishment. After midnight, the Voice turned off, so anything could happen. The chancellors always assumed the worst. Why else would someone stay out? Or at least that was the reasoning of the chancellors. But whatever Raaf chose to do to them still wouldn't be pleasant.

"No one will catch us out here."

Phoenix grinned. "You have a point. But who knows what we'll do after midnight. We could go crazy and murder the guards."

She stood and brushed off her skirt. "You don't honestly buy that bull that they feed you about what happens after midnight? Have you ever stayed awake?"

"Yes," he replied.

"Then you know you don't go crazy. You just think differently and nothing seems wrong."

"But the guard would notice if I wasn't there to get locked up, and I would be in serious trouble. Plus, it's not safe. You know this." It was true. Because the

Voice turned off, anyone could do anything without repercussion. As children, they were warned about the evil that lurked in the midnight hours.

"I know. I'm just not ready to go in."

"Me either. This was fun. Would you like meet again tomorrow?" he asked.

"I'd love to." She smiled at him, and he returned the smile. Her insides tingled. The things she could do with that boy after midnight. Thousands of thousands of kisses. She grabbed his hand and squeezed. He squeezed back without looking at her and then disappeared down the path.

Judging from the color of the sky, she had about twenty minutes. It would take her at least fifteen to get to her room. It was light enough to see outside, but inside the castle, it got pretty dark. Because of the constant sunlight, they didn't use candles often.

Zwaantie hesitated, wondering what she would do if she chose not to lock herself in her room. Hide out somewhere, probably. Those stories she was told as a child still lingered in her mind. After midnight she could be raped or murdered.

Time, Princess. It is time to go in. You don't want to be caught outside after midnight.

Zwaantie obeyed reluctantly. The headache wouldn't be worth it. She gathered her shoes and socks and meandered down the path barefoot.

As she turned the corner toward her room, she saw a guard marching down the hall locking doors. She hurried. The Voice urged her to run. She settled on a light jog. All over the kingdom, guards were locking doors of homes to protect the people from those who stayed out. It was the only time of day that the Voice couldn't protect them.

The guard waited by her door. "Cutting it a little close, aren't we, Princess?"

"But on time."

"Dangerous out there after midnight. People do crazy things."

The clock tower began its twelve o'clock strike. Zwaantie felt a change in the air. The sun had slipped into the gray, taking the Voice with it. The guard's eyes went ice blue, and he looked at her differently, like she was no longer a princess but a girl who was beneath him. The midnight hour had come. Zwaantie slid into her room, shut the door, and waited to hear the door lock from the outside. After a few seconds, it did, and she was safe from the night. From both the guard and herself.

Most nights Zwaantie stayed awake and contemplated all that was wrong with the world. Tonight, she just wanted to sleep. She searched for the laces in the back of her dress to undo it. Her fingers fumbled for a few moments and finally gave up. She crawled under the covers with her dress on and fell into a deep sleep.

Chapter 8

The Game

The next day Zwaantie woke feeling giddy. She'd never felt this way before. She clung to it, desperate for the freedom it promised. Falling for Phoenix was dangerous, but for now, she didn't care. She rolled out of bed and tried to ignore Luna's disapproving glare.

"Mud, grass, and sticks. How old are you?" Luna tugged the dress down and tossed it into a basket. Then she took in the bed.

"Next time you decide to go rolling around by the pond with my brother at least take your dress off before you get into bed." She pulled the cover over the grass and dirt on the white sheets. "I'll take care of this later."

"How'd you know I'd been with Phoenix?"

"Because he came home looking just like you. I'm not dumb."

"I thought you had your own house now."

"I do. But it's closer to the castle than mother's house, and so Phoenix stayed with us. He didn't think he'd make it home on time. Zwaantie, what are you doing?"

"It's not like we did anything. I was just missing my childhood. We played tag."

Luna sat Zwaantie down in front of the mirror and frowned.

"You know, we're not kids anymore. It's probably not a good idea to go sneaking around the woods together. Besides, I thought you were supposed to be with your mother and the lower queens."

Zwaantie spun around. Luna was trying to take away the only thing she had control over. Plus, they were growing up way too fast. They should do more running around in the woods. "That's ridiculous. There's nothing wrong with trying to hang onto our youth. In fact, you and I are going to dig out Sticks and Serpents and go play with Raaf and Phoenix this afternoon."

Luna motioned for Zwaantie to turn around, and continued her brushing. "Are you sure? I don't want you to be disappointed if Raaf says no."

"Wilma said that maybe I just needed to get him on his own for a bit. It's a good way to ease into a conversation. I miss him." She did. Part of her just wanted to see Phoenix, but she was also doing this for her brother. She needed him too. Maybe she could put her life back together on her own, and then she'd have allies to help her figure out how to avoid becoming queen. Raaf was an important ally.

"I know you do. Now come on, let's get you dressed, or you're going to miss lunch."

"Is it that late?"

"Yes. You know, when you become queen, you won't be able to sleep in anymore."

Every time Zwaantie turned around, someone was reminding her of her place. She was so sick of this.

"Hopefully I won't have to think about that for a long time."

Zwaantie arrived to lunch a little late. The lower royal families had gone home. Mother scowled at her.

"I expected to see you in my room last night."

Zwaantie picked up her napkin and spread it across her lap. "I know. I'm sorry. I closed my eyes for a few moments and didn't wake up until my door had been locked."

Mother sighed. "Zwaantie, you need to start taking more responsibility. You'll be queen soon."

Zwaantie didn't bother to argue. That was the problem. Mother couldn't see that she wasn't responsible enough to be queen.

Raaf had mentioned at lunch that his afternoon was

free and he was hoping to catch up on his paperwork, whatever that meant. Zwaantie planned on making him put away his paperwork for her.

An hour after they ate, Zwaantie and Luna stood at Raaf's door with Sticks and Serpents in hand. Luna knocked, and Phoenix answered. Zwaantie saw his face and had to suppress her smile.

"Zwaantie would like to talk to Raaf."

"Of course, come in. I'll go get him." He went through a side door. There were all kinds of hidden and side passages throughout the castle to make it easier for the royal family to get to their offices.

Zwaantie and Luna entered. Zwaantie stopped short. She hadn't seen his room since he'd returned. Before he left, it was decorated in blues and greens, and toys were scattered everywhere. Now it was stark white. Everything from the comforter on his bed to the stiff couches near the fireplace.

Zwaantie and Luna sat on the horribly uncomfortable couch and set the game on the table. Phoenix returned a few moments later and grinned at the game.

"Oh man. We haven't played that in years."

"I know. I'm going to talk Raaf into playing."

Phoenix met her eyes for a second. "I hope you're successful. Raaf could use a few more laughs."

Moments later Raaf collapsed into the chair

across from her. "A game, really?"

"I thought you could use a break."

His stony face changed into a grin. "You have no idea. You know what four years of training and a few days on the job has taught me?"

"What?" Zwaantie asked, her eyes flicking to Phoenix. She couldn't stop looking at him.

"Being grand chancellor is boring."

Phoenix chuckled. "Being your slave is no party either."

Raaf shoved Phoenix's shoulder. "I can give you more work if you want. Have you seen my shoes? They're filthy."

Zwaantie snorted. "Being queen will be duller. Have you ever been in on those monthly meetings?"

Raaf shook his head.

"Oh yeah, I didn't start going until after you left. Well, I'm sure you'll go now because the old grand chancellor always did. Not exciting in the least."

"I have to prod her to keep her awake," Luna said.

"What are you waiting for? Let's play," Raaf said.

Zwaantie opened the box with relief. Maybe she'd been mistaken on how much Raaf had changed. Raaf dealt out the cards. Zwaantie peeked over hers at Phoenix. His brow was furrowed as he looked over his cards. He was adorable when he was thinking.

They started to play. Zwaantie had picked this

game because it allowed for a lot of talk time.

"What exactly did you do in training anyway?" Zwaantie asked.

"I read a lot of books."

"Really, that's it? Why did you have to go so far away?" Zwaantie still didn't know where he'd gone. Only that letters took a week or more to get to her.

"I asked that question a time or two. The only answer they gave was that I would concentrate more if I didn't have any distractions. Most of the time, it was just me and a chancellor locked in a room. The lower chancellors rotated every week, and the grand chancellor came a few times a year. But I learned everything I never wanted to know about the Voice and Sol. Some of it was interesting, but most of it was boring."

"Tell us something interesting," Luna said.

Raaf set down his cards and tapped his chin. "Did you know that the Voice can actually force you to do something?"

"What do you mean?" Phoenix asked.

"Well, our only experience with the Voice is that it scolds and causes pain. But sometimes it will stop people from doing horrible things after they start. So if someone started beating someone, the Voice can force them to stop."

Zwaantie shivered. She hoped the Voice would

never force her to do anything she didn't want to do. That seemed dangerous.

Phoenix picked up a serpent card. "You know, no one actually knows what a serpent looks like, but I don't think this is it."

"Are you saying serpents are something different?" Zwaantie asked.

"Yeah, we had them in Stella, but they only come out after midnight." He paused for a second. "The Voice doesn't want me talking about that. Sorry."

Zwaantie rarely heard Phoenix or Luna voluntarily talk about Stella. She supposed Luna didn't remember much, but Phoenix might. He was two years older than his sister.

"Why did you come to Sol anyway?"

"Our dad died, and mom didn't have many skills. She failed out of mage school. Mom's sister was a trader and married a Solite and settled down here. She told mom to come on over, and she'd take care of her."

Luna stiffened next to her, and Zwaantie wondered how bad this story was going to get.

Phoenix set down a few cards. "When we arrived, we discovered she'd married a cruel man, and after a month, he threw us out on the street. We had no way to get food, and by then we'd been in Sol long enough that the Voice wouldn't let us go home. Mom had no choice but to become a slave."

Zwaantie felt sick to her stomach. She didn't want to know this story.

Raaf cocked his head at Phoenix. "How could he be cruel? The Voice wouldn't let him."

Phoenix sneered. "The Voice is not all knowing. There are a lot of things a person with a sadistic nature can still do."

"Like what?" Raaf asked. "The whole point of the Voice is to stop people from doing bad things. I just spent the better part of four years learning about this. It's not possible for someone to be evil."

"Yes it is. You're not allowed to starve your children, but you can give them only a tiny amount of food so they'll never feel full. I can't hit my sister, but if I were to tease her and play a little rough on purpose, the Voice wouldn't be able to tell the difference. Those kinds of things. Plus, all bets are off after midnight. The guards can lock you in your homes, but what happens behind closed doors stays behind closed doors."

Raaf frowned, and Zwaantie wondered what he was thinking. She'd known that was possible. She couldn't figure out why he hadn't. Maybe it was because she tested the Voice often. Perhaps Raaf never walked the line. Never tried to see what he could get away with.

Luna threw down her cards. Ten sticks and ten serpents. "Ha, I win."

They played three more games, and the conversation turned lighter. It was relaxing and fun. Zwaantie took every opportunity she could to watch Phoenix, and she noticed him doing the same. She hoped that no one else saw. She was falling fast.

Chapter 9

The Complication

Thoughts of Phoenix bothered Zwaantie all week. She kept losing track of what she was doing and couldn't stop thinking about the way his eyes met hers or the smile that formed on his lips every time they crossed in the hallway. This had never happened before. They'd met every night except one when he had to stay with Raaf. Was he thinking of her too?

She and Luna spent the day hiding out in Wilma's cottage sorting potions and cutting herbs. She didn't want to risk running into Mother and discussing her duties or the princes. Last night Mother had offered to travel to Haul to visit with the prince there. She said Raaf wanted to see Cornelia anyway. Zwaantie wasn't going to give Mother another opportunity to make her go away. She wanted to stay here in the castle where she and Phoenix had a refuge. A place to be together, but not together. He was on her mind constantly, and that unsettled her.

She couldn't shake her thoughts. After dinner, she practically ran to the rock by the pond. She beat him this time, climbing onto the rock and watching a couple swans in the pond. There was clean water just on the other side of the hedges, but the swans wanted to play in the dirty water. Maybe they were hiding from others as well.

She'd been so focused on the swans that she hadn't heard Phoenix arrive. He touched her shoulder, and she jumped, nearly falling off the rock. He grabbed her, wrapping his arm around her waist, and when they steadied, she found her face inches from his. His lips were so close. She leaned closer, wanting to feel them on hers, but he backed away.

She let out a breath of frustration.

"Are you okay?" he asked, his eyes serious.

She straightened her dress. "Yes. But you shouldn't sneak up on me like that. I nearly fell off."

"I wouldn't let you fall. How was your day?" he asked.

She shrugged. "Boring."

"Mine as well. Your brother spends more and more time alone."

"Don't a lot of people come to visit him to confess?"

"Yes, but he only takes confessions for a few hours a day. He spends time in the evenings with the guards, but that's it."

She grumbled. "He's doing all this grown-up stuff.

Soon I will have too as well. I'm not looking forward to that."

"I can picture it now. You in those meetings with all the lower kings and queens, bossing them around."

"Oh no. I don't want to attend those stupid meetings. Maybe I can delegate that to my husband." The word was out of her mouth before she could stop it. She would have a husband. She didn't want to think about a possible spouse. Because that person wouldn't be Phoenix.

Phoenix wiggled his eyebrows. "Any idea who it might be?"

"No. Not yet."

They both went quiet. She looked down and saw his hand splayed on the rock. She wanted to hold it. His fingers were long, and she wondered what they would feel like woven in with hers. This would be brave and daring, and she would risk a headache and a thorough telling off, but maybe, if she was careful, the Voice wouldn't even notice.

She moved her hand so their fingers were touching. He didn't move. This was a good sign.

"Have you seen Luna's new house yet?" she asked.

Phoenix nodded. "Yes. I stay there a lot. The beds are nicer."

Zwaantie slid her fingers across the top of

Phoenix's. Neither said anything for a long second. Then he flipped his hand over and wove his fingers into hers. A thrill buzzed in Zwaantie's chest.

She was surprised the Voice wasn't berating her. Physical touch was discouraged, but holding hands wasn't forbidden. She supposed the Voice could find nothing wrong with this.

"Princess, you know that I am a slave."

"Yes. I do."

"Then why do you..." His words trailed off, but Zwaantie understood. He couldn't say anything. He didn't want to bring their clasped hands to the Voice's attention any more than she did. If Phoenix made a big deal out of their hands, the Voice might decide it meant more.

"Because I like your hair. And you have nice eyes. And you're sweet and kind, and sometimes feelings can't be helped." She'd said too much. Any second now, the Voice was going to tell her that she wasn't allowed to say nice things to slaves.

He grinned. "No, I suppose they cannot. Can I ask how long you've felt this way?"

"Not long. Maybe just last week."

He laughed out loud. "Well, Princess, I can tell you I've felt this way far longer."

He looked deep into her eyes and brushed away a stray strand of hair.

"How long," she asked, her voice barely above a whisper.

He dropped his eyes. "I don't know. Since shortly before Raaf and I left. I thought of you constantly. I just assumed I'd have to watch from afar."

"You've never said anything before today. Why?"

"I'm a slave. You're a princess. It's treason."

He jerked his hand out of hers and gripped his head. Zwaantie placed her hand on his shoulders. "Are you okay?"

He took a couple of deep breaths and then shook his head, his dark curls flying around.

"I'm fine," he said, blinking his eyes. "That one hurt."

Zwaantie watched him carefully. "Did the pain go away, or will you have to confess?"

"It went away. I should be okay."

Zwaantie wondered how far this would go. She felt so powerfully about him in such a short time. Maybe the feelings would fizzle just as quickly. She hoped not. Her skin tingled at the possibilities. Their relationship would be forbidden by both the Voice and her mother. She didn't want to see Phoenix in pain. She had to find a way to make this okay, if not with Mother, then at least with the Voice.

She needed to know the rules. Was it actually wrong for her to love a slave, or was that just

Mother's idea? There was a difference between tradition and true right and wrong. Zwaantie had never thought about this before. It was time to find out.

Chapter 10

The Wagon

Zwaantie was on a mission. One that involved escaping the castle for a few hours with Luna, Phoenix, and Raaf. Things had been easier with Raaf since they played Sticks and Serpents, but she hadn't been able to spend a lot of time with him.

Slow down. This is not appropriate.

She stopped running and cursed the Voice for interfering. She settled on a brisk walk, her shoes clip-clopping on the floor, and ignored the slaves bowing to her as she passed. The castle seemed filled to bursting with them today. Odd.

She rounded a corner and knocked on a door. Phoenix opened it. Her lips twitched into a small smile. "I wish to see my brother."

Phoenix frowned. "Now's not a good time, Your Highness. Please come back later."

A high pitch wailing came from inside his room. "What's going on?"

"Just chancellor business, please come back later."

"No," Zwaantie said and pushed the door open.

Sprawled out on Raaf's floor was a merchant

child, probably around ten, flailing around, screaming. A woman, whom Zwaantie assumed was the girl's mother, hovered over her. Raaf ran into the room from a side door. He tried to calm the child, but she continued to flail.

"Speak, woman. What did she do?"

"She hit her father. I've never seen pain come on so fast. Help her, please."

"You lie. If a child hits a parent, they may have pain strong enough to confess, but not this. Tell me, what did she do?"

The woman pressed a hand to her forehead, and she sank to the floor.

"No, you don't," Raaf said, his voice rising. He was still attempting to calm the child, but wasn't having any success. "You need to tell me what she did."

Tears flowed down the woman's cheeks. "She picked up a butcher knife and tried to kill her father. The pain took her down before she could make contact." Zwaantie brought a hand to her mouth. She'd never heard of such evil from a child.

Raaf's mouth dropped open, and he stood. "Phoenix, help me bring the child to another room. Zwaantie, can you stay here with the mother?"

Zwaantie nodded. "Of course." She spun around to find that Luna wasn't with her. She'd forgotten she'd sent Luna off to gather a few things for their afternoon. Zwaantie guided the mother to the couch. Then she went to a side table and poured out a goblet of wine for the woman. She handed over the wine, and the woman took it with shaking hands.

"I'm sorry, Your Highness. I've imagined meeting you on many occasions, but never quite like this." The woman continued to tremble, her voice weak.

Zwaantie forced a smile. "Don't worry about it. Would you like to tell me what happened? Get it off your chest?"

Silent tears flowed down the woman's cheeks. "I've never seen Hilde behave like that before. She was so angry. We all were, but Hilde took it the worst."

"Why was she angry?"

"Hilde's the youngest and is a pretty little thing. She'll never understand what it's like to not be wanted. But her oldest sister, Ina, she just didn't stand a chance. We tried for three years to find a good match for her. But you know after twenty, the good ones are gone. We even searched for a farmer's son, figuring that would be better than nothing, but no one wanted her. She is too ugly. We had no choice."

Zwaantie couldn't understand what the woman was saying.

"What did you do?"

"We did what any parent does when they have an unwanted child. We gave her to the slavemaster."

Zwaantie's recoiled. This was unheard of. No parent would do that to their children for such a stupid reason. Maybe she wasn't telling Zwaantie everything.

"Was she a strain on your family financially?"

"No, but what else were we going to do with her? She's our responsibility until she's married. She couldn't marry. We had no choice."

Parents were responsible for the care of their children until marriage. If a child never married, they had no responsibilities. To turn your child to the slavemaster was beyond wrong. But allowed, according to the Voice.

They waited for what seemed like a long time but was probably only a few minutes. A knock came on the door, and they both jumped. Zwaantie cracked it open. She wasn't used to opening doors on her own.

"What's taking you so long?" Luna asked.

Zwaantie stepped into the hall. "Raaf is taking care of someone. I need you to run an errand for me though. Hopefully by the time you get back, Raaf will be done. Go to the slavemaster and inquire about a girl named Ina. Tell him I want her assigned to the castle. A good job."

Luna nodded and rushed down the hall.

Several minutes later, Raaf finally emerged with Phoenix, who carried the unconscious child.

The woman wailed and rushed to his side. "Is she okay?"

"Hilde will be fine," Raaf said. "She's exhausted, but I managed to convince the Voice to remove her pain. She will probably have a residual headache for some time to remind her of her extreme deed, but after a few months, it should go away."

Phoenix handed the child to the mother, and she staggered under the weight. Phoenix immediately took the girl back.

"Find a castle slave to carry her home. Then come back here," Raaf said.

Phoenix nodded and followed the woman out of the room. Raaf collapsed onto the couch.

"That was brutal, huh?" Zwaantie asked. Her mind was still spinning. She'd never realized Raaf's job could be so difficult. She wondered how often he was awakened or interrupted for extreme cases.

"Yep. First time I have had to deal with attempted murder. Normally they'd be executed. But I couldn't do that to a child."

"Was it hard to convince the Voice to let the pain go?"

Raaf shook his head, and Zwaantie waited for him to elaborate, but he didn't. She took a deep breath. If time wasn't so short, she wouldn't bother asking this now, but they'd already wasted a good half hour. Who knew much longer they had.

"The mage wagon is here. We're going to see the show. Do you want to come?" The mage wagon was one of her favorite things to see. They always did magic that was typically forbidden in Sol.

He wrinkled his nose. "No, why would I want to do that?"

Her stomach clenched. She and Raaf had always gone to see the mage wagon together. He lay on the couch with his eyes closed. His hair was a mess, his jaw still tense. He was probably still upset by the child. He could use the time to get out and relax.

"We always go together." The last time they went was right before he left for his training. That year the mages brought fireworks. Even in the bright light they were spectacular. Raaf chased her around with a sparkling stick, laughing. She missed his laugh.

"When we were kids. Don't you think you are a little old to be doing things like that? What will the people think, seeing their soon-to-be queen frequenting such a questionable venue?"

She shrank away, hurt. Sure, the Voice always gave small warnings when they got close to the wagon, but she didn't think it was that bad.

For a half second she debated starting the

argument they'd gotten into at dinner last night, the one about the virtues and vices of magic. If Raaf had been the heir to the throne, he'd rid the kingdom of all magic and seal the border so Stellans couldn't trade with them. Good thing she was the heir. That was one thing she was looking forward to. She'd allow more magic.

Time was slipping away. The mage wagon never stayed long.

"Can Phoenix at least come with us?"

"Yes, but act like a princess," he said with a glare.

He was in a bad mood. She stood and left the room before he said anything more.

She waited down the hall for Phoenix. He came around the corner, and Zwaantie couldn't help but smile. He was so handsome.

"Raaf said you could go to the mage wagon with us."

They took off down the hall, and Zwaantie resisted the urge to grab Phoenix's hand. The Voice would give her a thorough telling off, and she wasn't in the mood to listen to it and feel the pain that would follow.

Luna stood by the side doors with a basket under her arm.

"No Raaf?"

"Nope. Everything go okay with the slavemaster?"

"Yes. She'll be working as a serving maid."

"Thank you." Relief placated some of Zwaantie's guilt. It was strange, feeling guilty without the influence of the Voice. She wasn't sure why she felt guilty. It wasn't her fault the woman sold her daughter off to the slavemaster, but she still felt responsible for some reason.

They'd planned on walking to the wagon, but sitting just outside the front doors was a royal carriage, complete with a footman.

Zwaantie rolled her eyes. Raaf. He'd make sure she acted like a princess.

Fine. She put on her best smile and took the outstretched gloved hand of the footslave. They would arrive at the wagon with fanfare and announcement. They'd be lucky if it was still there by the time Zwaantie showed up. Certain magic was allowed in Sol, but the mage wagon always bordered on breaking the law. The mages wouldn't want the rulers of Sol watching them.

The wagon arrived with great fanfare and fun, probably so that all the merchants would know they were there. They came twice a year and negotiated with the merchants for food in exchange for potions and a few other things. The rest of the year, the merchants waited by the wall for unmanned carriages. They would unload the goods and fill the carriage up with food to send back.

They rattled along the cobblestoned street and passed small homes and farms. The horses frolicked in the fields, and the cows mooed unceremoniously, but the people on the streets dropped everything when the carriage approached, knelt, and pressed their faces to the ground.

As the carriage got closer to the wall of mist, the houses grew farther and farther apart. Farmers didn't like their cattle wandering too close to the wall between the two kingdoms. They disappeared too often. Sometimes because of their own stupidity and sometimes because of Stellan bandits. The wagon was set up in an empty field about a hundred yards from the mist. Zwaantie only saw the wall a few times a year. It always took her breath away.

The wall extended the length of Sol. No one ever found the end of it. Explorers tried on occasion, but none ever returned. The wall disappeared into the sky, inky black and swirling. Wisps of black smoke occasionally shot out about ten feet. If it caught a person, it would drag them into its depths and make them go mad with memories. Eventually, the mist would spit out those it captured, but they wouldn't have any memory of who they were or where they came from.

Stellans crossed the barrier, but only if they clung

to the Rod of Lost Memories so they wouldn't lose their way or spend too long inside. Solites never ventured to the other side. The Voice forbade it.

The sun was high in the sky when they arrived at the field. Though aside from the midnight hours when the sky went gray, the sun was always high in the sky. Sweat appeared on Zwaantie's forehead almost immediately. It was warmer near the border than by the castle.

The carriage stopped next to the edge of the field. Luna, Phoenix, and Zwaantie climbed down the stairs. Zwaantie sighed as she took the hand of the footslave.

People sank deep onto the ground as Zwaantie strode past. She wished she could hide amongst the slaves like Luna and Phoenix, but she was cursed with royalty.

The wagon in the center of the field appeared stranger than normal. A shimmering clear bubble surrounded it. People entered the bubble like it wasn't there. How odd. The Voice berated Zwaantie as she got closer.

Evil things reside in there. Go home.

"I'm not doing anything wrong," she said. Luna looked at her funny, and Zwaantie pointed to her head. Luna nodded.

True, but you are flirting with an act of

disobedience. Go home.

“How would you know? Now be quiet until you have something real to berate me for.”

Zwaantie walked straight through the bubble without hesitation, followed by Luna and Phoenix. She stopped short just inside, and Luna ran into her.

Everything was dark, and she couldn’t see. Fear clutched at her throat. She hated the dark. She inched forward and felt Luna grab for her hand. It was virtually silent inside the bubble.

After about thirty seconds, Zwaantie’s eyes adjusted and shapes appeared. It wasn’t completely dark. It only appeared that way because they’d come out of the sunlight. A small light ball hung in one corner, and thousands of other tiny lights were scattered along the bubble.

The wagon sat in the middle with a few magic lights floating around it. Luna gasped and sunk to the ground.

“Oh, stars,” she breathed.

“What?” Zwaantie asked.

Then she understood. The bubble was a replica of the Stellan sky. The stars glittered against the blackness, and the moon provided more light than Zwaantie thought was possible.

She sat on the ground next to Luna, her eyes wide, and let out a laugh.

"Luna, it's the stars."

Luna smiled.

Phoenix settled on the grass on Zwaantie's other side. She wanted to grip his hand, but she wouldn't risk that in public.

"I never thought I'd see them again," Phoenix said.

"I never thought I'd see them at all," said Zwaantie.

All around, people entered the bubble and had similar reactions. They fell to the knees, and mouths dropped open.

"It looks the same. I'd forgotten, but this brings back many memories," said Luna.

"Yes, it does. Do you ever want to go back?" Phoenix asked, his shoulders relaxed and a lazy grin on his face.

She snorted. "Yeah, right. Like that would be possible."

Zwaantie's stomach churned. They weren't allowed to go home. Ever. Of course she wasn't allowed to go over there either, but at least she was in her own home.

"Is it like this in Stella?" Zwaantie asked, pointing at the stars.

"Sort of. These are so close. In Stella, they feel much farther away. But the patterns are the same. Look, there's Orion's belt. He was always my favorite gaw—I mean star."

"Is it this quiet in Stella too?" Zwaantie wasn't used to the peace.

Luna scrunched her nose. "It's not that quiet right now."

Phoenix pointed to his head. "She means in here."

He was right. It wasn't physical noise Zwaantie couldn't hear, but the Voice was gone. She scrambled to her feet. It was common knowledge that the Voice didn't exist in Stella. The hair on her neck and arms stood straight up, and she shivered. If they could create a way for Stellans to be in Sol without hearing the Voice, then they could attack Sol. Sure, it was a weird magical bubble, but that didn't mean they couldn't use the magic.

A couple of hundred years ago, the Stellans tried taking over Sol, but as soon as they crossed the barrier, the Voice commanded them to stop. They stood there like cows waiting for the butcher. The Solite soldiers slaughtered them, and an uneasy truce formed. Now Stellans only crossed the border when they needed food.

Zwaantie left Phoenix and Luna watching the stars and approached the wagon. Most of the magic the Solites purchased from Stella consisted of potions. Spells didn't work unless they were first cast in Stella. Unless a spell was in the form of a potion or attached to an object, it wouldn't work in Sol. The wagon usually pushed the boundaries of magic allowed in Sol. The Voice allowed potions, but discouraged them. If someone tried anything more, they'd be in pain for a week from the Voice. Only the bravest Solites purchased spells from the mage wagons. But this was also where the majority of their medicines came from, so it was allowed.

Zwaantie couldn't find a mage anywhere. She hadn't planned on buying anything other than potions, but now she wanted to make a very big purchase. Low voices floated around from the back of the wagon, and she stopped to listen.

"We can't sell these with her here. She'll go snitching to the king." The voice was soft, female.

"We spent months perfecting them. They are our money makers this year." This came from a male with a deep voice.

"Let's figure out what she wants to buy and get her out of here so that we can start trading," the female said.

Zwaantie peeked around the corner to see if she could make out what they were arguing over. What could they possibly want to sell that was so bad they didn't want her to see? Zwaantie came every time they were in town. That was no secret.

The male mage took a handful of necklaces from

the female and shoved them in his pocket. Zwaantie hurried around the wagon.

"I would like to purchase one of those," Zwaantie said.

Both mages looked up with eyebrows raised. The male recovered first. "One of what?"

"Those necklaces."

He reached for a different necklace from the wagon. It was made of jewels and glowed. "This necklace is a rare piece of work. It will light up any dark room."

Zwaantie placed her hands on her hips. "Not that one, one that you have in your pocket."

"I'm sorry. I don't know what you are talking about." A bead of sweat appeared on his forehead, but he kept his body relaxed. He was good.

"You shoved a bunch of necklaces into your pocket. I want one of those."

He reached for his pockets and turned them inside out to show her that he had nothing. Sneaky little devil. She'd lost this one. But then she remembered why she'd come looking for them in the first place.

"I want to buy the stars. I'll give you one year of royal food."

"This dome? You want to buy the dome?"

"Yes. And I'll give you an extra half year if you

come set it up for me."

He glanced at his companion. She shook her head. "It's not for sale."

"Do you know who I am?"

"Of course, Your Highness, but this is just an illusion. It only works for a short amount of time. By the time we got it to your home, it would be all but gone. And we don't feel right taking such a large sum of food for something so fleeting," the girl said with a sigh. She meant she didn't want to get her tail handed to her when she came back to town. "However, we do have something else that might interest you. Something that will last longer."

She snapped her fingers, and a table appeared in front of her. Zwaantie's heart stopped for a second. "You can't do magic in Sol."

The mage's face fell, but she didn't miss a beat. "Of course not. But the illusion allows us to perform magic under the dome. Again, it's temporary. The table, Your Highness."

At Zwaantie's feet sat a low table, oblong in shape. The surface gleamed black. It appeared to reflect the dome above with sparkly stars and a crescent moon.

"It's a reflecting table?" Zwaantie asked.

"No, it's a replica of the sky. The moon will change shape with the actual moon."

Oh, this was good.

"Yes, I'll take it. Half a year of royal food?"

"Three quarters," countered the male mage.

"Done."

"But we'd like to be paid in merchant food," he replied. Royal food was higher quality but by using merchant food, they'd get more.

"Of course. Phoenix," Zwaantie called.

"Yes." He appeared at her side almost instantly.

"Go fetch the footslaves to gather my new table. It's time to go." She would inform the trade master of her deal, and they would make sure the food was delivered throughout the year.

Zwaantie looked over her shoulder just before she left the bubble. Both mages watched her. She was insanely curious what those necklaces were that they were going to sell, and she worried what it meant. Stella usually didn't pose a threat, but today not only did they find a way to turn off the Voice, but they were selling objects they did not want her seeing. Perhaps Stella was more of a threat than she originally thought.

Chapter 11

The Task

The Voice looked around the crowded workroom and at the discarded lists he'd picked up from the box outside his door. The room was tall, three or four stories. Glowing orbs hung in the air like thousands of tiny suns, filling the space all the way up to the ceiling. The orbs ranged in size from pebbles to the carriage-sized bright white ball that hovered a few inches off the ground. A few tables were scattered along the walls, piled high with papers. The orbs moved out of the way as the Voice moved through the room.

This was the only place in all of Sol where spells could be cast. Though the magic was quite different than that of Stella. Stellan magic was wrong and went against nature. Through the Voice, Sol's magic ensured the obedience and passivity of the people. It provided order.

The Voice controlled it all. The ball in the center, the one the size of a carriage, managed the collective conscience of Sol, but the other smaller ones influenced individuals. Earlier today the Voice had been given a list of people who needed whispers added to their balls, but the list lay on the table forgotten. During the years the Voice had been in control, not one other person had ever found or entered this room. It should've been impossible. But today, the Voice had a visitor.

She delivered a life-changing message that was as vague as it was apocalyptic.

"Zwaantie," the Voice commanded, and Zwaantie's orb, along with those who were close to her, zoomed toward him.

The Voice studied her glow. She wielded more influence than she realized. She was beloved by those around her, but the Voice made sure she stayed humble. She'd been a challenge to restrain, but the Voice had done a good job growing her into the right kind of queen for her people. One that listened and was not overly confident. The Voice loved Zwaantie more than she knew.

Now she threatened everything.

Though the visitor had been cryptic, one thing she'd made clear was that the Voice would die.

Unless Zwaantie died first.

The Voice did not want Zwaantie to die, but sometimes sacrifices needed to be made to save the kingdom. If the Voice had an orb, it would be among those closest to her. Zwaantie's death would be difficult, but the Voice would do what was necessary.

Murder would be unheard of in Sol. The Voice would have to be careful so that it would not appear as if the Voice lost control of a person. Zwaantie's death would have to be carefully planned. The Voice moved around the orbs that surrounded Zwaantie. It would also have to be someone who was compliant and eager to follow the Voice's command.

The Voice smiled at the orb that circled closest to Zwaantie. That one would be perfect.

Chapter 12

The Problem

On the carriage ride home, Phoenix chatted easily about his memories of Stella. Under normal circumstances, Zwaantie would've been all over their conversation, but right now she was distracted. She stared out the window as the small houses and shops passed by. This was her kingdom. One she would be in charge of someday. A task she didn't want. Especially now.

The Stellan mages found a way to do magic inside Sol. They said it wouldn't last long. But they could do it. And if they could do magic inside Sol, then they could attack. Casting the spell was an entirely different than potions. It wasn't possible in Sol. At least not until now. And those necklaces—they must've been something evil as well. What was so bad about them that they thought she'd tell her father?

Once back at the castle, the footslaves took her table to her room. Luna and Phoenix followed her through the front doors. Zwaantie normally took the back doors, but she had to talk to Mother and Father, and this was the easiest way to get to them. She held up her skirts and marched up the stairs. As she neared the top, slaves opened the doors, and Zwaantie strode through the empty grand hall and out a side door to the meeting room.

Her mother and father would be in there taking care of something mundane like how to increase the production of chicken eggs. The hallway outside the meeting room was crowded with slaves, their bands reflecting under the sunlight that streamed in through the skylights. She found Ariel standing next to the door.

"What's going on?" Zwaantie asked her.

"It's the first of the month."

Oh Sol, Zwaantie had forgotten. Why in the dark didn't the Voice warn her? It was usually so good at reminding her of things she didn't want to do. She was late, probably by a couple of hours. Raaf could've reminded her too. Brat. He probably wanted her to miss the meeting, thought it would be funny. And here she was thinking he'd gone stuffy. She'd pay him back for this one for sure.

Zwaantie turned to Luna. "How's my hair?"

Luna smoothed out a few stray strands while Ariel brushed dust off Zwaantie's dress. Phoenix smirked next to them, and Zwaantie had to resist sticking her tongue out at him.

"I'll see you later," Zwaantie said to Luna, but her eyes were on Phoenix.

A slave opened the door. Zwaantie pressed her lips together and entered the room with her head held high.

A group of nearly twenty people sat around the large oval table. The men stood as she walked into the room, and she racked her brain for an excuse. They would demand one.

She took her place next to her mother and avoided her eyes. Father and Raaf sat on her other side. The rest of the people at the table were lower kings, queens, and chancellors of various villages. Every month they gathered at the castle to discuss problems and solutions. Zwaantie hated these meetings because they were insanely dull. She thought she was too young to attend, but Mother insisted.

Speak, demanded the Voice.

Every eye in the room was on her. She'd hoped they would just continue like she hadn't come in extremely late. But she had no choice. Zwaantie stood.

"Please forgive my tardiness. A group of Stellan mages entered our borders a few hours ago, and I went to investigate."

A cough came from a few chairs over, and she

knew it was Raaf trying to cover a laugh.

"And what did you find?" asked Mother. A few snickers came from around the table. No one expected anything good out of Zwaantie. She was the disobedient daughter of the high king and queen. The one who would rather run with slaves than other princes and princesses. The one, who, when she thought no one was listening, sounded like she came from the streets of Stella. But she blamed that one on Mother, who gave her Stellan playmates when she was young. What did Mother expect? Today though, Zwaantie would surprise them all.

"They have discovered how to turn off the Voice."

A gasp escaped most of those who sat around the table.

Raaf recovered first. "That is impossible. The Voice rules over Sol. It cannot be turned off. It is what keeps us safe. If they can turn it off, then they will invade."

"I witnessed it for myself. They created a bubble, and the minute I stepped within the bubble, the Voice went silent. Everyone noticed. The Voice can summon them here to witness if you don't believe me. But if you do believe me, we need to decide how to fix this."

Mother stared at her, stunned. But being the high queen, she went into action mode. "And how do you propose we do this?"

"We start by having spies at the border, and the next time a mage enters, we question him until he explains."

A voice came from across the table, the lower king of Ghrain.

"You had the authority to arrest them. Why didn't you?"

For a half second Zwaantie had thought that maybe she could do this. Be queen. But once again her inadequacy was thrown back in her face. She could've brought the mages in to be questioned by Raaf. Another reminder of why she wouldn't be a good queen.

"I don't know," Zwaantie said, sinking down into her hard chair. She kept her head up because that was expected her, but she wanted to bury her face in her hands. She kept her eyes trained on the tapestry of an apple orchard hanging above the king and queen of Slonce.

The lower king sniffed. Conversations flared up around the room. Zwaantie wallowed in her own self-pity while the rest of the leaders of Sol decided how to protect her country since she obviously couldn't. Maybe now Mother would entertain thoughts of Zwaantie giving up the throne.

After the meeting, Mother caught up with

Zwaantie and Luna in the hallway.

"Tonight you will be seated next to the prince of Ghrain."

Zwaantie groaned.

Stop that. She's your mother. You will listen to her.

"Yes, Mother, but last time was a disaster. I don't expect tonight to go any better."

"Well, try harder this time, and so help me, if I hear one word about mooing, I'll have your tail. The prince is the one who suggested we increase the guard at the barrier."

Anyone could have suggested they increase the guard. Even the slaves would've thought of that. Zwaantie rolled her eyes.

Stop being disrespectful.

"Yes, Mother."

The prince from Ghrain was older than her by about six years. He was good looking and charming. But also condescending.

That evening, Zwaantie settled into her chair before the prince arrived. Luna stood behind her, smoothing her hair as he took his seat with a flourish.

"I see your mother made you sit with me. Are you finally deciding to choose a husband?"

"My mother thinks so." Zwaantie looked around. Where were the drinks?

"Well, you will obviously be picking me. I don't see that you have other options."

What an arrogant jerk.

"You are mistaken. I have plenty of options."

"Where? Sonnenschein? I heard you ran him off awfully fast. I'm not quite as easily deterred."

Zwaantie almost asked him to moo for her, just to prove a point, but decided against it. She needed wine and fast.

A serving slave stood before her, pale as the clouds in the sky. The tray the girl held shook. "Wine or water?"

"Wine, please." Zwaantie reached for the wine, but before she could take the goblet, the slave collapsed onto the floor, convulsing. The cups clattered to the floor, the wine leaving a dark stain on the stone.

Zwaantie was out of her seat in seconds. She knelt by the girl's side, the floor cold underneath her knees. It was a slave she was unfamiliar with. She'd probably seen her around the castle before, but didn't know her name. The girl's face was pale, and her lips had a strange blue tint. Blood trickled out of her mouth. Zwaantie touched the girl's neck. Nothing.

Luna knelt down next to her and put her arm around Zwaantie's shoulder. "Zwaantie? Are you okay?"

Zwaantie shook her head.

"Move, girls." Wilma stood next to them. They scooted over but did not stand.

Wilma moved her fingers over the girl's lips and opened her eyes. Zwaantie did not look. She was already afraid of the nightmares that would come from this experience. This poor girl had just died right in front of her. Why?

Dead," declared Wilma to the waiting crowd. "You," she said, pointing at a slave boy. "Go fetch a couple of diggers."

Zwaantie still hadn't moved. "What do you think happened to her?"

Wilma shrugged. "It's hard to say. From the looks of it, she bled internally. It could be any number of things. Especially if she had trouble earlier and didn't tell anyone. Death is the way of the world, and it happens, even to the young."

A few minutes later, two men arrived in dark brown tunics and took the girl away. The dinner conversation had been hushed during the ordeal, but no one made to leave. As soon as the diggers and the girl were gone, Mother motioned for the slaves to serve them dinner. Zwaantie looked at her mother, hoping against hope to convey that she wanted to go to her room. But her mother just nodded to the prince behind Zwaantie, which she took as a sign that she was to take her seat at the table.

Luna pulled Zwaantie up. Zwaantie's legs shook as Luna helped her to her seat. After she sat, she placed her hands in her lap and stared down at them. Those hands had just touched a dead body. What if she was contagious and Zwaantie would be the next to go? No one else seemed concerned about that. Another slave girl brought her a warm wet cloth, and Zwaantie used it to wash her hands.

She glanced at the prince. "Excuse me. I'm afraid I've lost my appetite." She rushed from the room, Luna on her heels.

She collapsed onto her couch.

"Are you okay, Your Highness?"

Zwaantie shook her head. "A girl just died right in front of me."

"Yes. She did."

"Did you know her?"

"A little. We weren't close."

"Everybody acted like we're just supposed to continue with dinner, like nothing was wrong."

Luna shifted. "I suppose they thought she was a slave, and it didn't matter."

Zwaantie cringed. "That's not right."

"It is the way of life. Why don't you take a bath, and I'll brush out your hair? That always soothes you."

"Yes, that would be nice. Thank you."

Luna had just finished helping Zwaantie put on her night dress when mother entered.

"You left early."

"I did. The death was too much for me."

Mother sank down onto the couch. "You know, when you're queen, you will have to carry on even if you run into hard situations. That wasn't smart running out like that. You'll make the people believe their queen is weak."

Zwaantie was tired of being reminded of her duties. Tired of thinking of marrying a man she'd never love, tired of being queen, and she hadn't even become one yet.

"What if I don't want to be queen?" There she finally said it out loud.

Take it back. This is treason.

A hand flew to her mother's breast. "How could you say that?"

Zwaantie exhaled and twisted her hands together. "Because it's true. I don't want to be queen. Raaf can have the throne. Please, Mother, you must see that I will not be good at this."

Treason. There is only one punishment for traitors. Zwaantie expected a pain in her forehead after a declaration like that, but none came.

"Raaf is already the grand chancellor. Besides, Sol

demands that as the oldest heir, you be queen. If you choose not to, you will be sentenced to death. There is no abdicating."

"What?" Zwaantie had never heard this before. No one ever talked about what would happen if she didn't take the throne.

"I may be queen, but we answer to a higher power." Mother pointed out the window to the sun. "You are called by Sol to become queen."

"And if I run away?"

STOP THIS RIGHT NOW. The pain began then, just behind her eyes.

"Then that is between you and Sol, but I doubt you'd survive more than a couple of weeks. This is ridiculous."

This would be irrelevant if Stella found a way to take over. Then she'd be a slave like Luna and Phoenix. Though that might fix her problem. Maybe Zwaantie shouldn't have warned her mother and father about the way the Stellan mages turned off the Voice.

She shook her head. What was she thinking? Sol was her home. She should be concerned about her people, not helping the enemy.

Mother didn't say another word as she swept from the room. Luna sat on the couch with her and held her hand.

"I never knew," she said.

"I know. I'm sorry. I just feel so trapped in my life."

Luna gave a snort. "I can relate."

"I shouldn't compare my life to yours. I'm sorry. It's just that I want to be a midwife. Not queen."

A knock came at the door. Luna answered it. Phoenix poked his head in, and Zwaantie couldn't help her smile.

He sat in the seat Luna had just vacated, and he took her hand in his. "Are you okay?"

"Of course. It was strange watching that slave die, but I'm fine. How did you get away?"

"Raaf sent me to check on you. He wanted to come himself, but he was tied up. I was happy to help."

Luna hovered over them, glaring. "You should leave. I need to help Zwaantie get ready for bed."

Phoenix didn't say anything. He just brushed a strand of hair out of Zwaantie's eyes. She shivered at his touch and let out a sigh.

The door clicked shut, and Zwaantie met Luna's eyes. Her face was hard. "You're playing with fire."

It sure felt like it. Zwaantie's chest burned every time she saw him. Luna was worried about her brother, and Zwaantie supposed he could get hurt in this, but the truth was that she was the one who would likely end up in flames.

Chapter 13

The Plan: Part 1

The Voice was trying hard not to lose his temper. He stood among his glowing orbs and muttered to himself. The orbs would absorb some of his words, and right now a very confused farmer was being told he was an idiot and he had to try harder next time. But at this moment, the Voice didn't care. He slammed his fist down on a long table that sat next to the wall. A few lists slid off the table. He picked them up and read the first one.

The following people of Haul need to have their guilt removed.

Sjabbo, farmer, confessed to the sin of moving his fence and encroaching on another's property.

Mina, shopkeeper, confessed to the sin of purposefully keeping the change she owed her customers.

Bastiaan, student, sixteen years of age, confessed to kissing a girl.

This was his job. He was to remove the guilt whispers from their orbs so they could be free of the pain associated with it. There were a half a dozen lists sitting on his table, and he hadn't attended to a single one. He clutched at his hair. How was he supposed to think about these mundane things when he was about to lose his power because of the princess? He had to get rid of her so he could focus on doing his job.

Shoes clattered on the floor in the hallway behind him. He was about to have another visitor.

The door opened, and in she strolled. He left the orbs behind him so none would pick up the conversation. The woman's face twisted into a sneer, and she wasted no time getting in his face.

"That was stupid and foolish. You could've exposed the plan to kill her before even getting a decent shot at it. You're lucky most of the kingdom doesn't recognize the signs of poisoning. Not to mention the fact that an innocent victim died. You can't let that happen again."

"Relax, woman. It was just a slave girl. You don't seem that concerned about Zwaantie's life. Why are you worried about a slave?"

She took two deep breaths and then snapped her fingers. Every orb in the room blinked out.

The Voice's stomach clenched, and his hands went ice cold. This woman just turned off the magic of Sol. "Turn it back on." He couldn't think of anything else to say. Not until the orbs were glowing again. He fought the rising panic in his chest.

"No. Not until you hear what I have to say. If you fail, this is the result. Everything goes away. No more magic, no more Voice, and chaos in the streets. I have seen all the possible futures. The only ones in which the Voice still remains in power are the ones where Zwaantie dies. Unless you want this to be a reality, she must die, and you cannot make any more foolish attempts like today. Find a way to do it now, because the beginning of the end starts tomorrow."

She snapped her fingers once again, and the orbs glowed, like they'd never been turned off in the first place. The Voice sank to the ground, grateful a crisis had been averted. The old woman put a gentle finger on one of the orbs nearest her, and the Voice resisted the urge to swat her hand away. He'd never even touched them.

"Do you ever wonder how it all started?" she asked.

"How what started?" He couldn't concentrate on the conversation. His mind was still with her declaration of all the possible futures. How powerful was this woman anyway?

"This room. The Voice."

She wasn't making sense. "I am the Voice."

"Of course you are, but you haven't always been."

"I know that, but there is no beginning. The Voice

originates with the creation."

The woman cackled. "Oh, you fool. It began as a spell. A good one too. I was there."

The Voice furrowed his brow. This couldn't be true. He was the Voice of God. This woman was blasphemous.

"You lie."

"I do not. Let me show you. Call to you the orb of the Bakker child. He's an infant and won't remember or understand our words."

The Voice didn't want to listen to her, but something about the way she spoke made him follow her directions.

He called Philip Bakker's orb to him. His mother, father, and sister's orbs flew with it, but he waved them away. The orb floated between him and the old woman. Her eyes sparkled as she examined it.

"Now before I show you, I'd like to know how much you understand. How does the Voice work?"

"The Voice exists inside the head of every Solite."

"But are you present?"

"No, I simply give the orb instructions, and it acts of its own accord. I would go mad if I was in everyone's head all the time."

"Very good. Essentially, you don't know what anyone has done until the chancellor delivers you names of those who need guilt and pain removed."

"Right, and I can choose whether or not to remove that pain. Once an instruction has been given, only I can modify or change it. I can also choose how strict the Voice is with individuals. Slaves are dealt with most severely while the royal family is given some leniency."

"How do you force someone to do something?"

"I have to allow my consciousness to enter their orb, essentially seeing everything they are doing. In that instance I have total control over their actions if I choose. I can do that to all of Sol at once if I wish."

But he wouldn't ever enter the entirety of Sol. After forcing someone to do something, he always felt exhausted and a little dirty inside. He didn't like being in other people's heads. He didn't know what would happen if he tried to enter the collective conscience.

The woman waggled her finger in his face. "I wouldn't try that if I were you. You have a better understanding than I thought you did. Now to the creation."

She brought her hands together on Philip's orb, and it disappeared into mist.

"What have you done?" The only time orbs disappeared was when someone died. "Did you just kill him?"

"Relax. He's fine. He simply has no 'Voice' at the

moment. He doesn't need one. Now watch."

She spun her finger in a circle. Silvery threads dripped out and formed a new ball. She stopped moving her finger, and the orb floated in front of his eyes.

"There, Philip has a new ball. No gods involved, just magic."

Chapter 14

The Plan: Part 2

Zwaantie was alone. It didn't happen often, but Luna was off getting one of Zwaantie's dresses fixed, and Mother was having lunch with her sister. Zwaantie didn't like alone time. It allowed for too much thinking. She picked up a tapestry she and her mother had been sewing together and worked on a tree in the corner.

She had a lot to think about. Phoenix had stolen her heart, and she didn't even know that was possible. The thought of marrying anyone else filled her soul with dread. She wanted Phoenix. Committing to him meant marriage and kids were impossible. If they ever had children, they'd be born slaves. Because if anyone married a slave, their children were automatically slaves.

Zwaantie thought through the possibilities. She could refuse to marry, and she and Phoenix could just be lovers. She snorted. Yeah, right. The Voice would never allow it. Maybe love was possible in the Stellan fairy tales Ariel told her when she was younger, but in Sol, love was only possible in marriage.

She could become a slave. But who would do that? Besides, then she'd have to face the wrath of Sol. That wasn't possible.

If only the Voice wasn't so obnoxious. Zwaantie sat up straighter. That was it. The Voice. Her brother was the grand chancellor. He could talk to the Voice. He could fix this. Zwaantie dropped the tapestry. She couldn't believe she hadn't thought of this earlier.

Pick it up.

She stared down at the tapestry lying on the floor. It seemed such a dumb thing to berate her for. She had grand problems, and the Voice was telling her to clean up her messes. She picked it up and slammed it on the table.

She strode quickly down the hall and knocked on her brother's door.

Phoenix opened it. A smiled formed on his lips as he looked her over. She kept her face straight. He would probably be angry with her when this was over.

"I need to speak with Raaf."

"Of course, Princess, come in."

Raaf was sitting on a chair staring into the fire. She sat across from him, and he jerked his head up.

"I need your help," she said.

Raaf picked up the glass in front of him and took a

sip. "You always need my help."

"You love me. Right?"

"You're my sister. Why would you ask a question like that?"

"Because I have to know I can trust you."

Raaf set his glass down and leaned forward. "You know you can trust me. I've never told Mother and Father anything you've done. And, Zwaantie, you've broken more rules than anyone I know. I don't know how you aren't in here pleading with me every day. Or is that what you need? Have you finally done something so bad that the pain won't leave?" He cocked his head and gave her crooked grin.

She scowled. "No, my head is fine. But you can't tell anyone. I'm actually here to try to prevent a scolding from the Voice."

Raaf waved his hand. "Continue. You have my word."

Zwaantie let out a deep breath. "I'm in love."

Phoenix stood behind Raaf, his hands clenching the back of Raaf's chair. Zwaantie met Phoenix's eyes. He glared at her and shook his head.

Raaf shifted in his chair, and Zwaantie refocused on him. This was for the best even if Phoenix didn't think so.

He picked up his glass and took another sip. "It's about time. Mother will be thrilled."

"It's more complicated than that. Mother won't approve." Zwaantie clutched her hands together. She was scared of what Raaf's reaction would be. Phoenix's as well.

Raaf gave her a small smile. "Give her a little credit. She just wants you to be happy."

Zwaantie forged on, knowing if she didn't, she'd never get it out. "But I'm in love with Phoenix."

Foolish notion, girl.

Raaf dropped his glass, and it shattered. Phoenix hurried to clean it up. Zwaantie couldn't see his face, but his shoulders were tense and his motions jerky. Was he angry with her? She was trying to fix this.

Raaf covered his eyes and then ran his hand slowly down his face, pinching his lip. He closed his eyes and gave his head a slow shake. "Zwaantie. I can't help you. You have to know that. You've put yourself in an impossible situation." He rubbed his forehead.

Zwaantie wrung her hands. The anxiety in her chest was building. "But there has to be a way. We could run away. I could become a slave. We could find a way to remove Phoenix's bands. There has to be."

You've gone too far. Respect the system.

"Removing the bands isn't possible. As for you becoming a slave, only Mother and Father have access to the bands, and you know that won't happen. If you run away, the Voice will make you come back."

Zwaantie jumped. This was the opening she'd been waiting for. "But you can fix that, can't you. You talk to the Voice. Tell him what we need. He listens to you." The Voice was strangely quiet. She expected something more.

Raaf let out a snort. "It doesn't work like that."

"What do you mean? You tell the Voice all the time to remove pain and guilt."

"Actually, I don't. You know, grand chancellor is little more than a pretty face."

Zwaantie frowned. "What do you mean?"

"I mean, I listen to the people's pleadings, write down their requests, and leave them in a box outside the Voice's chambers. Every day the lists are gone. Most of the time the Voice does what I ask, but sometimes it doesn't. I have one man who visits me every day begging for the pain in his head to be removed, but the Voice never listens. I have other duties as well. Ones that don't involve the Voice. The guards answer to me, and I interrogate those caught in possible crimes, but my interaction with the Voice is about the same as yours."

"But the little girl."

"In emergencies, I can slide a note under the door.

But even then, I think we got lucky."

Zwaantie sat back in her chair defeated. She thought for sure this would work. Phoenix took his place behind Raaf again, stony faced. He wouldn't look at her.

"Well, what do we do now?" Zwaantie asked.

Raaf craned his head around to look at Phoenix, but Phoenix just stared at the door.

"I don't know. Move on. Your love story won't have a happy ending. I'm sorry. I wish there was more I could do to help. Besides, Zwaantie, you know as well as I do, that it's your responsibility to become queen. Anything else would be dishonorable."

Zwaantie wanted to argue. What about responsibility to herself? Since when did honor trump everything including her own happiness?

"Will you keep our secret?"

"Of course, but I would highly advise you to cut it off. This won't end well."

Phoenix was already at the rock when she arrived. She climbed next to him, but he made no move to touch her.

"You should've talked to me first," he said as she settled herself.

"I thought Raaf could help us."

"But he couldn't. This is a mistake, Zwaantie. I think we need to stop seeing each other."

Zwaantie put her hand on his tightly crossed arms. He didn't react. "No. Please. You know I how feel."

"Raaf is right. This will not end well."

Zwaantie felt like she was about to cry. She hadn't realized how much he meant to her. The thought of just ending it broke her up inside. "We can figure out something." They had to.

"No, this is too risky."

Zwaantie laid her head on his shoulder. "I'm willing to risk anything to be with you." A small pain started in her forehead.

Remember your place, Princess.

He scooted away from her. "No. This has to be the last time."

Zwaantie felt something break inside of her. "Phoenix, please."

"Don't make this any harder than it has to be." His face softened. "Tell you what, let's make this count. Your turn to catch me."

Without a word, he jumped off the rock and ran into the woods. Zwaantie worried that if she didn't go now, she'd never see him alone again. She raced after him, trying not to think about this being the last time. She refused to believe it.

It took her a while, but eventually she caught him. Somehow she ended up pinned underneath him with his fingers tickling her ribs. At first she laughed, but her feelings quickly changed from amusement to desire. She loved the way his fingers pressed into her sides and lingered on her stomach. Phoenix leaned down and whispered in her ear.

"You need to keep laughing or else..."

She was certain he was about to say, "Or else the Voice will know." So she laughed, but her heart wasn't in it. Especially when he looked at her with serious eyes. She knew his feelings changed for her as well.

When she couldn't stand it anymore, she wiggled out. "We should go in."

"We should."

They were silent as they traipsed to the castle. The sky was rapidly turning gray. This was the closest she'd ever cut it. She couldn't hurry though. She had too much on her mind.

The thrill of desire crawled up her spine. It settled into her chest and abdomen. She'd never felt this way about anyone before. The need to be close, to hold, to touch, to kiss. Phoenix squeezed her hand and went his separate way. She watched him saunter away for a long minute. This was the end. She fought tears as she stalked to her room.

She got to her door at the same time as the guard. His normally friendly eyes had taken on a hard stare. That was strange. The midnight bells had not begun to ring yet.

She pushed on her door, but the guard grabbed her arm and spun her around. Pressing her against the wall, he had his sword against her throat. Zwaantie couldn't breathe. The guard's eyes bored into hers. She tried to move, but found herself paralyzed with fear. She couldn't scream. The sword was pressing too hard. He was going to slice open her neck. This wasn't possible. She had so much to live for.

The confusion in the guard's eyes was clear. She clutched at the sword cutting her hands. But the guard held it fast.

"Why?" she whispered.

A shadow appeared around the corner just as the clock began its nightly midnight strike. Phoenix rushed for the guard and jerked him away. The guard dropped the sword and looked at both of them with bewilderment.

Phoenix shoved her into her room, and she clutched at him. "No, stay with me."

"Yes," said the guard. "Stay and protect her."

Zwaantie didn't understand what was going on. Ten seconds ago, this man wanted to kill her, and now he was telling Phoenix to protect her. Zwaantie tugged at Phoenix's hand and pulled him in. The guard slammed and locked the door. They wouldn't be able to get out again until morning.

She felt her neck. There was a dent where the sword pressed, but at least he hadn't drawn blood. She might have some bruising in the morning, but nothing worse than that. Her hands were another story. Blood dripped onto the floor.

"Sit," Phoenix commanded and ran for her washroom.

He came back with a few wet cloths. He gently washed her hands and wrapped them with dry ones.

"Are you okay?" he asked, his dark eyes full of concern.

"That depends. Physically, I'm fine, but my guard just tried to kill me. Why would he do that?"

"I don't know. Did you notice how he stopped when the bell rang?" The bells signaled the midnight hours. As soon as they stopped ringing, the Voice turned off.

Did that mean that the Voice was trying to kill her? Why? No. That was absurd. The Voice kept them from doing bad things.

"We'll have Raaf deal with him tomorrow. Maybe he'll have some insight on what happened. Let's get you to bed."

Zwaantie glanced sideways at him. "You know, there is no Voice."

She wrapped her arms around his waist and pushed herself into him. The sheer physical contact was exhilarating. Zwaantie could stay there all night.

He held her tight. She brushed one of the curls out of his eyes. They sparkled at her.

"We should still get you to bed."

"You're coming with me."

The torment in his face was heartbreaking.

"What? The Voice won't know."

"But I will, and I will ache for you afterwards. Zwaantie, if I'm to have you, I want you all the way. I can't have you tonight and then never again."

Zwaantie's breath caught in her throat, and she didn't know what to say. "Where are you going sleep?"

"I'm not. I'm going to make sure some murderous guard doesn't try to break in here."

"Okay, I'm going to change."

Zwaantie's hands shook as she changed into her night dress. Phoenix stood at the door and watched her with smoldering eyes as she climbed in bed.

"Come tell me a story," Zwaantie said.

He chuckled. "I'm not your nursemaid."

"I still want to hear a story. Something from Stella."

He sat down on the edge of her bed. "I don't remember much from Stella. I miss the smells though. I lived on an island, and the smell of the sea was my favorite."

"What does it smell like?" She'd heard of the sea, but had never seen it before. It was on the other side of the mist.

"A little like salt, but different. I don't know. Someday see if you can buy a shell from a trader. They smell like the sea."

Zwaantie gripped his hand, and he squeezed back. "Tell me something else."

"The food was awful."

"Really?"

"Truly. They can't grow fresh food, but you already knew that. But imagine eating fruits and vegetables that are days or weeks old. They use magic to preserve it, but it still doesn't taste like the food here."

"Will you lay with me? Just until I fall asleep. Please."

He ran a finger along her jaw. "Yeah, scootch over."

She pressed her back into him, and he pulled her tight against his body. As she drifted off, she realized she'd never been more comfortable. How could she ever sleep without him again

Chapter 15

The Visitor

Zwaantie woke the next morning to a squeal. She sat straight up and found Luna with her mouth hanging open. A hand snaked around her waist and pulled her tight. Oh no.

She pushed at Phoenix's shoulder. "Wake up."

He groaned and then slid out of bed. Then he fell to the floor holding his head.

Zwaantie jumped up and hovered over him. "What's the matter?"

Luna came over and tugged at his arm. "What's he doing here? Help me get him up."

Zwaantie pulled at his other arm, and he stood, but was hunched over holding his head.

Luna glared at Zwaantie. "In less than ten seconds, tell me what happened."

"My guard tried to kill me. Phoenix rescued me and stayed with me to make sure the guard didn't return."

Luna creased her eyebrows. "Okay, I'm going to take him to Raaf. You stay here and don't go back to bed."

Zwaantie paced back and forth in front of the fireplace and waited for Luna to return. Why did the Voice punish Phoenix, but not her? She didn't understand what was going on. Especially with the Voice. Luna returned and clicked the door shut.

"Will he be okay?" Zwaantie asked.

"Raaf was going to the Voice to plead for him right away, but it's up to the Voice."

Zwaantie collapsed into a chair next to the fireplace. "It's all my fault. He was going to stand by the door all night."

"Don't say anything else. He had a completely good reason to be in your room. The Voice will see that."

"Why are you here so early?" Zwaantie asked, realizing that the day just began. She was going to crawl into her bed and sleep for another three hours. Luna went and opened the curtains, sending sunlight streaming into the room.

"Because someone is coming to visit the castle."

"Well, whoever they are they can come back later. You know I don't function until after noon. Close the stinking curtains." Zwaantie found her covers, pulled them to her neck, and put a pillow over her face.

"Your mother is going to be here in fifteen minutes. I should've had more time, but your guard was missing, though now I understand why. I had to go track down the head guard for the keys. Now, unless you want to explain to her why your hair is a mess, you'll get up."

Zwaantie sat up, and the bright yellow duvet settled around her waist. "What does she want?"

"To make sure you are prepared for the guest."

"Did the head guard say what happened with my guard?" She rubbed her neck, the memory of the steel fresh in her mind.

"He killed himself. It happens after midnight sometimes."

Zwaantie didn't know how to process this new information. Something must've been wrong with him.

"He tried to kill me."

Luna dropped her voice. "Let's not tell anyone. We don't want to draw attention to Phoenix. Raaf will keep the secret."

"What secret?" Zwaantie's mother asked from the doorway.

Zwaantie jumped and blushed because she stood in only her underdress. Zwaantie's mother hadn't seen her this undressed since she was five years old. Zwaantie spun around so her mother couldn't see the mess of grass in her hair.

"Oh, just that I stayed up too late. I'm not used to being up this early."

Mother crossed the room, sat in a chair by the fireplace, and studied her. Zwaantie shifted her feet. Her underdress wasn't sheer, but it was pretty close. Plus, without a dress on, her breasts were plainly visible.

"You are to be on your best behavior today. Or I will see that you marry Prince Moo-For-Me. Do you understand?"

Mother had never threatened Zwaantie before. Whoever was coming had to be someone important. But Zwaantie and her family were the most important people in Sol. The lower kings and queens visited all the time.

"Who's coming?" Zwaantie asked.

Mother played with the lace on the edge of her collar, her jaw tense. "A high prince. I want you to wear your red dress, the one with the sequins. And Luna, will you put her hair in a fancy braid? He should be here within a couple of hours."

Luna curtsied. "Of course, Your Majesty."

Mother got up and nearly swept out the door before what she said registered. "Mother, wait!"

"What?" she asked in exasperation.

"What do you mean, a high prince? Raaf's the only high prince in Sol."

"Yes, I know that. The high prince is from Stella."

Zwaantie sank down onto her bed. Luna sat in the

chair Mother just vacated.

"Stella," Luna uttered, her eyes staring off into space.

"Stars. That prince has stars." Zwaantie pulled her bright yellow blanket up to her shoulders and wrapped it around herself. "Why do you think a high prince from Stella is coming here?"

Luna pulled her off the bed. "Your guess is as good as mine. Maybe he's coming to seek your hand in marriage." Luna's eyes sparkled, and Zwaantie knew she was joking, but that was actually one of the more sane reasons. He had another thing coming if he thought she was going to marry him.

"This is unheard of." The royal families hadn't spoken to each other in over two hundred years. The only Stellans they ever had contact with were traders.

Luna led Zwaantie to a steaming tub of water. "Get in. We'll talk while I'm fixing your hair."

Zwaantie undressed and slipped into the water.

"Mother can't possibly want me to marry him. The people from Stella are barbarians. They don't wear decent clothes, and they have no rules. And no sun. How could I live over there? I want to see the stars, but not at the expense of the sun."

"Even if he is seeking marriage, your mother wouldn't hear of it. She just wants you to behave while he is here. Believe it or not, I think your mother might feel threatened by his presence. Stella leaves us alone most of the time. What if his visit isn't friendly? After all, they do know how to turn off the Voice."

Zwaantie hadn't thought of that. "But then why does Mother want me to behave?"

"I'm not even going to answer that."

Zwaantie's face was scrubbed clean, and then she stepped out of the tub. Luna dressed her in a bright red dress and pulled the laces tight. Then she braided Zwaantie's hair.

The trumpets blared to announce the arrival of a visitor, and Zwaantie made no move to go down to the great hall. She wanted the prince to meet Mother and Father first. Truthfully, Zwaantie was hoping she wasn't necessary for this visit. She didn't want to meet him. What if Mother made Zwaantie marry him? Then she would leave Sol. And Phoenix.

No, she couldn't make her do that.

"Should we go?" Luna asked, startling Zwaantie out of her thoughts.

"No, we'll wait until we are summoned."

Luna and Zwaantie didn't talk while they waited. Thoughts buzzed in Zwaantie's head about why a prince from the dark side, would be in Sol.

He could show her the stars. In spite of herself,

she was excited to meet him. She wondered if he were old or young. It was always hard to tell with princes. Would he be dressed like them or would he wear garments from his own kingdom? People in Sol believed that if no skin was shown, the temptation was less. But Zwaantie disagreed. The more that was covered the more curious she was to see what was underneath.

Luna told her that in Stella they wore whatever they wanted, and sometimes they didn't wear anything at all.

Ten minutes later Raaf appeared in the doorway with Phoenix at his side. At least he wasn't still racked with pain. He didn't even glance at Zwaantie. She hoped he wasn't ashamed of the previous night. She certainly wasn't. She warmed at the thought of his arms around her.

Raaf scowled. "What are you doing? The prince will be here any minute."

"Waiting to be summoned. I'm not that excited to meet him."

"None of us are, but Mother wants you next to her when they arrive."

"Fine."

Luna fussed with her hair a little more, and then they followed the boys to the entrance hall. What would the prince think of her home? Was it like his in Stella? They'd never had a high prince set foot in their castle before. Would he find it impressive or lacking?

The grand hall was wide and the ceiling tall. Mother and Father sat on thrones directly across from the enormous front doors. Sixty guards lined the path from the door to the thrones. Twice as many as normal. Zwaantie wasn't the only one skeptical of this dark prince.

Zwaantie stood next to Mother, with Luna taking her place behind them both, next to her own mother. Raaf and Phoenix went to stand by Father. Behind Father stood Pieter, tall and stoic. A few of the lower kings and queens had many personal slaves, but in the capital city they didn't believe in extravagance. One or two was sufficient. That left the rest of the slaves to attend to the needs of the kingdom. They took care of the roads and kept the streets clean of debris and sewage. They prided themselves in the cleanliness of their city.

The doors opened just as Zwaantie took her place next to her mother.

Chapter 16

The Prince

Two men entered and sauntered up the path to the thrones. They didn't seem awed or nervous of the guards. A little too cocky for Zwaantie's taste.

Both men were dressed identically. They had on dark pants with leather boots. They wore white billowy shirts that opened at the neck with a necklace that rested on the hollow of their neckline. It was a simple necklace, with no jewels. Just a silver disk attached to a leather thong. They wore bright multi-colored vests over their shirts.

Just before they reached the stairs to the thrones, they stopped and bowed. It became clear who was the prince and who was the slave. While the prince bowed deep and low, the slave was more cautious. He eyed the guards next to him with suspicion, and he never took his hand off the hilt of his sword. This was no ordinary slave. He was also his guard. A good one from the looks of it.

The prince rose from his bow and looked at Zwaantie's father.

"High King Geert, High Queen Janna, I bring the

greetings of my father, High King Ajax. He wished to come himself, but found that he's unable to get away from his current duties. I hope you will forgive his absence. High Princess Zwaantie and High Prince Raaf, it is a pleasure to meet you."

His voice was rich and lilting. The speech was obviously rehearsed, and he appeared to stumble over the names. The smile never left his dark face. She could see the similarities between him and Phoenix. They had the same devastating smile, rich caramel skin, and dark piercing eyes. But the prince's face was a little sharper. His hair was spiking instead of long and curly. He was definitely striking. Cow poop. She was hoping he was old or ugly.

He bowed once again, a short quick bow, and then spoke. "I am High Prince Leo, the fifth son of High King Ajax of Stella. I have come to see if it would be possible to join our kingdoms."

Father glared down at him. That was a bold statement for a prince in foreign territory. "How exactly would we join our kingdoms?"

His eyes met Zwaantie's. "Through marriage of course. I have no kingdom of my own. Marriage would create a partnership that I think we have both longed for."

Luna sucked in a breath, and Zwaantie flicked her eyes to Phoenix. He stood expressionless, but Raaf was frowning. Zwaantie's heart raced, and her palms began to sweat. She had no idea how her parents would react to this. Would they force her to marry him?

Father continued to glower at the man. Zwaantie let out a breath of relief. This was absurd.

After a long beat, Father waved his hand. "We have no desire to join with Stella. Zwaantie will be marrying a Solite prince."

For once Zwaantie didn't want to argue with him. She didn't want to marry a prince, but one from Stella sounded downright terrifying.

Leo appeared confused. "Did the princess not send a message stating they were desperate for medicines? If Zwaantie and I join in marriage, then we could have free and open trade."

Father stroked his beard. "We would be open to exploring additional trade agreements, but marriage to my daughter is out of the question."

Zwaantie let out a breath. She was in the clear. She watched the prince for a reaction. His face fell slightly, but he forged on.

"Very well. May we stay and discuss possible agreements? I will not be able to finalize anything, but after our discussions, I can take the agreements to my father." He flicked his gaze back up to her again. She averted her eyes. What was he doing?

"Of course. Where is the rest of your party?" Father asked.

Leo grinned, once again looking at her instead of Father. "My guard, Hunter, is the only one who accompanied me. We like to travel light. We hope you will be able to accommodate us. Also, we brought gifts from our home. Do you have servants who can help us fetch them from our carriage?"

Father snapped his fingers, and ten slaves appeared. They followed the prince's guard out the front doors. The prince looked around the great room, examining the tapestries and windows. He glanced at Zwaantie a time or two, but always averted his eyes when he caught her staring back. He was quick to agree to the trade possibilities, but he didn't seem to keep his eyes off of her. Perhaps he wasn't easily deterred. This could be a problem.

She took the time to study him. His angular face was different from theirs. The people of Sol were more round faced and jolly looking. His eyebrows were thick and dark, and he had an unbelievable amount of eyelashes. His eyes were a deep brown. In Sol, their eyes were usually blue or green. Occasionally gray, but brown eyes were rare.

The guard returned, and the slaves followed, carrying large trunks.

Leo opened the first trunk and took out a bottle.

"For the queen, I bring new medicines to better the health of your people. You will find that they are most effective in curing minor diseases and discomforts. There are also potions to enhance beauty, not that you need those." He grinned and closed the trunk. Two slaves lifted the trunk and placed it in front of Mother. She thanked him with a smile and raised her eyebrows at Zwaantie. Zwaantie gave a sharp shake of her head and watched as her mother stared at Leo. Was Mother considering his proposal?

The prince opened another trunk. This one was long and slender.

"For the king, I bring magically enhanced weapons." Leo pulled out a sword, and Father's eyes went wide. "This sword will never dull or chip. It is razor sharp and will slice through any opponent with ease. There are twenty of these."

Father gave Leo a rare smile. "Thank you. That is most generous. You know the way to a king's heart."

Oh Sol. Now Father was having second thoughts as well. If Prince Leo kept this up, they'd be forcing her hand within a day.

He replaced the sword and pulled out a small black box. He held it up for Father to see. "This is one of our newest inventions, a backsnipe."

Father pursed his lips. "That is no weapon. It is

just a small box."

Leo grinned.

"Ah, but it is indeed a weapon. It performs much like a crossbow. Do you see this small button?"

The king nodded.

"When I press this button, the bolt will shoot out from the end and will pierce whatever I aimed it at. We are working on accuracy spells, but haven't perfected them yet. Right now, if you are a good shot, this would be the best weapon you've ever used. May I demonstrate?"

The king whispered to a slave. The slave scurried from the room and came back carrying a pedestal. He set it down by the door and placed an apple on it.

The prince pointed the small box at the apple and pushed a button. A six-inch bolt shot out of the end of the box. It went through the apple and lodged in the door.

A collective gasp filled the room. We had no weapons like that. Stella would slaughter them in a war. Leo turned to Father who clapped his hands.

"That is extraordinary. We shall go hunting while you are here. I want to see those in action. Also," he said, waving over a slave. "Go down to the kitchens and tell them we have a rare opportunity to impress the Stellans. I want a grand lunch."

Zwaantie looked at Mother, who still studied the

prince with an intense gaze. Zwaantie wondered why no one else was suspicious. For years she'd heard how horrible the people of Stella were, and now here was her father and mother treating them like exalted guests.

The prince gave a small bow and put the backsnipe into a larger box.

"There are ten of those. May you use them wisely."

The prince opened a third, smaller trunk—about the size of a large jewelry box.

"I had heard Prince Raaf became the grand chancellor. This is a weighty position that requires great wisdom and carries responsibility."

He removed a leather throng like the one he wore.

"This disc is imbued with much powerful magic. In Stella, we all have them, and each is unique to the wearer. Mine protects me, and also increases my ability to observe, as I am an academic mage. I'm constantly looking to learn new things. We modeled yours off our head mage's disc, as she is the closest thing we have to a chancellor. When you wear this, your decision-making skills will be improved. We have created twenty so that you may share them with all of your lower chancellors."

The Stellan prince approached Raaf and handed him the necklace. Raaf put it on. He looked at the prince in awe. Now he would want her to marry Leo as well. This prince was making a very good impression on her family, but she wasn't convinced. Not yet.

"Finally, for the princess. It was difficult for me to know what to bring, having never met you before, but I had my sisters' help. First, I present you with a necklace that carries an amethyst, the gemstone of your birthday. Our magicians imbued it with many protection charms. While you wear it, you can never be harmed." He paused for a moment, putting the necklace back its box. "This was my choice. My sisters, on the other hand, insisted I bring you dresses."

He lifted one out. The material flowed across his hands like water. But it was missing many important pieces. Like sleeves. And the neckline plunged down so far that her cleavage would show. No one but Luna and her mother had ever seen any part of her breasts. Leo was not going to change that now.

Filthy dresses. Don't even think about wearing them.

For once, Zwaantie agreed with the Voice. She gathered her skirts together and got ready to depart. She couldn't stay here anymore. This prince came waltzing in here asking for her hand in marriage and presenting her gifts she could never accept.

Zwaantie spoke. "High Prince Leo, it was a

pleasure to meet you. But I'm afraid I'm not interested in your dresses. Now if you'll excuse me, I have a headache."

Zwaantie fled from the room, Luna close on her heels. She didn't bother to look at Mother before she left. Zwaantie didn't want to see the disappointment on her face.

Zwaantie had no intention of leaving her room again that day. She didn't have a headache, but she could pretend. Sleep would be wondrous. Maybe Luna could even find some of that magical medicine the prince brought.

Luna caught Zwaantie before she climbed into bed and wrapped Zwaantie in a hug. Zwaantie froze. There were times where Luna forgot she was in Sol and not Stella. Luna's instinct was to comfort Zwaantie, which she did a lot when they were kids, but she'd withdrawn since she became Zwaantie's slave instead of her playmate.

Luna whispered fiercely in Zwaantie's ear. "Are you okay?"

Zwaantie shook her head. "They all loved him. I know Father said I didn't have to marry him, but he's charming them. Did you see how Raaf was drooling?"

Luna pulled back and laughed. "Then Raaf can marry him. Sit," she said, pointing to Zwaantie's couch. "I'll change your sheets, and then we can get you into bed."

Zwaantie sat and stared at the star table. The moon was in a crescent shape and moved slowly across the table. For years Zwaantie had dreamed of traveling to Stella and seeing the stars. She wanted to see what Stellan magic was capable of too. But her dream was always to travel there, never live. Never leave her own home and become part of Stella. In spite of her annoyances with the Voice, she wanted to stay in Sol, marry Phoenix, and live on a farm.

In Stella they had magic. No need for fireplaces or lamps. They had blankets that warmed you and bright lights. But no sun. The dark terrified her.

"Come on, Princess, let's get you to bed." Luna undid Zwaantie's laces and helped her out of the dress. Zwaantie closed her eyes and pretended to sleep. A few minutes later she heard rustling at the door.

"She is asleep, Your Majesty. Her head ached terribly," Luna said. Zwaantie couldn't have asked for a better slave. Luna would do just about anything for her.

"Wake her up. She's never embarrassed me quite as badly as today."

"The princess is rather difficult when she's woken up. I can send her to you as soon she wakes."

"Luna, who am I?"

"The queen." Her voice quivered.

"Wake up my daughter, now, or you will be dismissed and will have to work with the sewage slaves."

Luna would never work the sewage route. Zwaantie sat up.

"I can hear you, Mother. What do you want?"

Mother crossed the room in three angry strides. Her face was beet red as she thrust it into Zwaantie's.

"How dare you. That is a high prince from Stella, and you...you..." Spittle landed on Zwaantie's face as Mother struggled to find the word.

"I rejected him, Mother. I'm sorry. You said I didn't have to marry anyone I didn't want to. He repulses me." It was a lie, but she needed to be dramatic for her mother's sake. Zwaantie kept her voice deliberately calm. Mother lost her temper occasionally, and if Zwaantie yelled back, it would just make things worse.

Mother's face softened, and she sank down on the edge of the bed. "Did you not hear your father? You don't have to marry him."

"But you were so excited by the things he had. I've never seen you look at a prince like that. How long will it be before you decide he's a good match?"

Mother stroked Zwaantie's cheek. "Oh dear girl. I don't want you to marry him. Not at all. We do need the things Stella can give us though, and this is the first time in centuries that we've had an open conversation with any member of the royal family. This will be a good thing."

Zwaantie relaxed just a little. "Thank you, Mother."

"But it is rude that you walked off like that. Especially after your father completely shut him down on his proposal. If perhaps we could announce your engagement, then Prince Leo will understand and be more open with our agreements."

"To who?" Zwaantie didn't want to think about this. She couldn't even wrap her mind around marrying someone. She was quickly falling for Phoenix, but marriage seemed so permanent. Especially since she'd never be allowed to marry him.

"There are four eligible princes. Pick one."

"What? Mother, no." She didn't know what she'd been expecting to hear. But she hadn't expected her mother to have an answer ready.

Mother's face hardened. "Zwaantie, I don't get it. What do you want?"

"To not think about marriage for a long time. Then in five or ten years, I want to marry for love." Zwaantie thought about telling her about Phoenix, but she could still see the fire in Mother's eyes and knew she'd never go for that.

"Fine. Then you will be Prince Leo's escort while he is in town. Show him the villages. Be good company. He plans on staying for two weeks. You may rest until dinner, but then you will come and be pleasant."

"Why? I don't want to." Everything about this prince made her nervous. She wanted to stay as far away from him as possible.

"Because after you left, he requested you to show him around. I think he thinks if he can spend time with you, you will choose to marry him even though your father said no. This is important."

Zwaantie gripped the sheets in her bed. Perhaps Mother and Father would force her to marry him in the end. He was from Stella though.

Mother left with one more disapproving glare.

"Luna, would you go find me some medicine? Something that will make me sleep."

"Of course."

A half hour later Zwaantie was lost to dreamland. No more thoughts of darkness and a loveless marriage.

Chapter 17

The Wall

A hand roughly shook Zwaantie out of her peace.

"Zwaantie, wake up. Wilma needs you. Now."

Zwaantie jerked awake and stared into the fearful eyes of Luna.

"What time is it?"

"Four-thirty. Come quickly. I have your brown dress ready."

Oh. No. The brown dress could only mean one thing.

"But I'll miss dinner. Mother is going to kill me."

"Well, then she is going to have to kill you. Wilma needs you. Perhaps you'll be done by seven. You'd be late for dinner, but you'd still make it."

"You know as well as I do that babies aren't born in three hours." But Zwaantie dressed quickly and followed. They found Wilma in her cottage bustling about gathering materials.

"Three women," she shrieked. "Three decided to have their babies now. I don't have six arms. How do they expect me to do three?"

"I'm here, and so is Luna. We'll both take

someone."

"No, I want you girls together. Another midwife agreed to help too. She's already on her way to the VanDykes. You will take Mrs. Jacobusse. She's already had four babies. This one should come out easy."

Zwaantie had helped deliver Mrs. Jacobusse's last baby two years ago. She was quiet. Zwaantie liked that in a delivery. The problem with Mrs. Jacobusse was the distance. She lived out by the wall. They'd never make it home in time for dinner.

The delivery went fast. The baby popped out just after nine-thirty. Still too late for dinner, but Zwaantie could make an appearance and appease Mother.

Luna followed Zwaantie to the door of the small house.

"Are you sure you can clean up on your own?" Zwaantie asked.

"Of course. Will you be okay walking by yourself?"

"Why wouldn't I be?"

Luna shrugged. "Because you're a princess. It's rare for you to be on your own without me or a guard. Or Phoenix." She smirked.

Zwaantie ignored the remark. "Exactly. I'm not by

myself often. I'll enjoy the walk. I'll see you tomorrow."

There weren't many houses out this far. Zwaantie stepped out of the stifling house, and she glanced at the inky blackness of the border between Stella and Sol. Stars, it was big.

Instead of walking toward the castle, she felt drawn to the wall and its whispers. She stood about twenty feet away and listened. The whispers were fragments of conversations and thoughts with no coherency whatsoever.

"The cow, he ran away. I swear it."

"My love. She died."

"What happened to the food? We had so much a few days ago."

Zwaantie didn't know what to make of the conversations. She took a few steps closer and listened some more.

"The pain. I just want it to go away."

"It's so hot."

"I didn't mean it."

A few steps more, and the Voice began its coaxing.

Get closer. You know you want to. Add your own voice to its whispers.

Zwaantie stopped abruptly. "You've always told me to stay away from the wall."

That was before. This is now. Go, step into the

darkness, and you will hear them all.

The breeze shifted, and her hair fluttered in her face. She brushed it away and took a few steps closer. "But that would be suicide."

Maybe, maybe not. But don't you want to know what the whispers are saying? Don't you want to understand?

Not really. She also didn't want the wall to grab her, steal her memories, and spit her out in a permanent state of amnesia.

Zwaantie couldn't figure out why the Voice was now encouraging her to go inside the swirling depths.

Go. See what it will tell you.

Zwaantie shook her head and closed her eyes. "No. I will not."

Yes, you will. Go now.

Zwaantie's head pounded with the disobedience. She took a few steps back from the wall. Tendrils of smoke reached for her. One encircled her wrist, and she heard a small child crying. Its cry was soft at first and then turned to a wailing. Zwaantie jerked her hand back, and the smoke withdrew into the wall.

GO NOW. WALK INTO THE WALL.

Zwaantie clutched her head. "NO! I WILL NOT!" She screamed louder than she had ever screamed before. The Voice went silent. She let go of her head.

That had never happened before either—the Voice going silent. She stood tall and looked at the wall defiantly.

"You lose," she said.

She trudged to the castle, tired, and arrived home just after eleven. She'd missed dinner.

The whole exchange with the wall made her wonder what the Voice was up to. Why would it coax her into the wall instead of warning her to stay away? Where the Voice came from was a mystery. She'd asked her mother when she was child, but Mother only responded that the Voice was Sol, telling her to be a good girl. Zwaantie doubted Raaf even knew.

Perhaps this was what Mother meant about Zwaantie not being able to escape her duty as queen. Did Sol know she wanted to abdicate and decided to put an end to her before she could do any more damage? Did Sol sense the intent of her heart?

No, the Voice couldn't do that. It could only react to spoken words or actions.

Zwaantie stopped just outside the palace door, realization dawning. She had spoken the words out loud. She told her mother she didn't want to be queen.

Chapter 18

The Surpise

Bright light hit Zwaantie's eyes, and she blinked a few times.

"Seriously, can't I sleep in?" She rolled over and tugged her duvet over her eyes.

"Not when there is a prince from Stella here. You'll just have to get used to the idea. I managed to smooth things over with the queen last night, but she said that you will be showing the prince around Sol today." Luna pulled the cover down.

"Thank you for helping me."

Luna sighed. "I'm used to it. What happened last night anyway? I made it home before you did, and I know for a fact you weren't with Phoenix because he was with Raaf until late."

"I got distracted on my way home." Zwaantie's stomach clenched. The Voice tried to kill her last night. This was the third time someone tried to take her life. At first she had thought it was a fluke with the guard, but now she was thinking it might be more than that. Maybe the slave girl was poisoned, and that poison was meant for Zwaantie.

She shivered and looked at Luna. She wanted to talk to someone, but didn't know who she could trust. She wasn't sure she could even speak the words out loud. Especially if it was the Voice who wanted her dead. She brushed her hair out of her eyes with shaky hands and tried to act like everything was normal.

"What's on the schedule for today?" Zwaantie asked.

Luna bustled about, seemingly unaware of Zwaantie's worries. "You are taking the prince for a walk around the village to show him how we live. Your mother made me promise to talk to you about being charming and not obnoxious."

Zwaantie stuck her tongue out at Luna.

Luna laughed and continued to blather. Which was fine, because as long as she talked and didn't notice Zwaantie was still in bed, the longer she could lie there. If she just stayed here, would she be safe. Was anywhere safe?

Luna threw off the duvet, and Zwaantie curled into herself. "It's cold."

You must get up. You have work to do.

"The water in your tub is hot. Go." Luna pointed to her bathing area. Zwaantie sighed and shuffled to the tub and sank into the steaming water. While Zwaantie soaked, she heard Luna rustling through something. She poked her head around the shade.

"Why don't you wear one of the dresses the prince brought you?"

Luna held up a short yellow dress that wouldn't go farther than mid-thigh. The skirt flared out and had something underneath that made it puffy. The top of the dress was even less sensible, with a neckline that plunged and sleeves that would barely cover her shoulders. While it was pretty, there was no way in the dark that she would put that on.

"You are joking, right?"

She wiggled her eyebrows at Zwaantie. "Phoenix would choke if he saw you in it. Maybe then he'd actually kiss you."

Zwaantie splashed water toward her. "How do you know these things?" Zwaantie's face burned. She did want Phoenix to kiss her, but she didn't realize Luna knew.

Luna ignored the question. "Start your scrubbing. I'll try to find something more suitable for you to wear."

"Something not out of that trunk."

Luna dug around the trunk for a while, gave up, and pulled out one of Zwaantie's yellow dresses. She'd always liked it because it felt sunny.

After dressing, Luna braided her hair, and Zwaantie ate a quick breakfast. Then they went down to the entrance hall.

The prince was already there, dressed exactly like he had yesterday, except he wore flimsy shoes that left most of his feet bare. Crazy boy. Didn't he know that his feet would get soaked in shoes like that? The streets were always wet. Not to mention the dirt and filth. Eww.

Zwaantie kept her eyes trained on the people around her. Could the gardener want to kill her? Or the maybe the woman out beating her rugs. It could be anyone. Except the prince. He'd arrived after the guard had tried to kill her, so it couldn't be him.

He bowed, and Zwaantie inclined her head.

"Princess," he said, taking her hand. "You look lovely this morning."

"Thank you," she replied. She thought about giving him the same compliment, but didn't want to encourage him. Though she was certain he didn't want to kill her, she still didn't want to marry him. They left the castle via the front door, Luna and Hunter following a few feet behind.

As they meandered down the road to the village, Zwaantie wondered what he thought of their town. Was it different from his?

"Your mother tells me that last night you helped deliver a baby, and that is why you missed dinner."

"Yes." Zwaantie noticed everything about the

village. The small houses, the cobblestone streets, the slaves and guards who hid just out of sight. What if another guard tried to kill her? Would someone stop them?

"Why do you deliver babies? Isn't that what healers are for?"

"In Sol we believe in being productive members of society even as royalty. My mother likes to sew, my father is an expert with a bow and arrow, Raaf cooks. I decided to train as a midwife. I find the work quite rewarding."

She wished the world was different. That she could be a midwife for real. What a simple life she'd live.

"I would imagine it would be frightening."

"How so?"

"You don't have magic. Don't some women die in childbirth?"

"Sometimes, but with the magic potions we get from Stella, we have less death then we used to. Do your women ever die?"

"Rarely, though occasionally a woman will give birth after midnight. Most of the time they are safe, but every once in a while, one dies. We consider it a great tragedy when that happens."

Zwaantie creased her eyebrows. "How is midnight different in Stella? Here the Voice turns off. But you have no Voice."

"Our magic disappears. It's quite frightening actually." His hands were in his pockets, but his shoulders were tense.

"Then I suppose it's not that much different from Sol at night then."

He gave a tight smile. "Sort of."

This early in the morning, there were slaves everywhere. They were picking up the trash, sweeping the cobblestones, and cleaning windows on the shops. Zwaantie probably should've waited a few hours before venturing out. She wanted to show the prince what it was like when everything was sparkling and brilliant. Not half done.

Each person they passed stopped whatever he was doing and bowed.

"Are your people always this respectful?" Leo asked, watching a slave to his left.

"Yes. Aren't yours?" Quite frankly, it was annoying. Just once she'd like to be able to walk down the street and not have everything stop dead.

He hesitated for a second, like he was debating whether to tell her. "No, they only bow when they come to the castle. Out on the street we are just like any other person. I like it. I can go to the store or a club without being harassed. I usually take Hunter with me for safety, but most people treat me normal."

Zwaantie didn't know how to respond. No one, except for Luna, Phoenix, and Wilma, had ever treated her like a normal person. Most wouldn't even talk to her. Even when she was delivering their babies, they are all "Sorry, Your Highness."

"Must be nice," Zwaantie said.

"It is."

A slave dashed in front of them to pick up a piece of discarded fruit. Zwaantie hadn't been paying attention and tripped over the slave. The prince caught her, and Zwaantie couldn't help notice a whiff of citrus and coconut. He smelled like summer.

In a flash, Luna had the slave by the ear and dragged him to the edge of the street. She would give him a tongue-lashing, and he would never step in front of royalty again.

The prince stared at Luna and the slave for a moment with a frown. Zwaantie wondered what he was thinking. They walked on and passed the bakery with an incredible aroma of bread and cakes floating out.

"Does your village look like this?" Zwaantie asked.

"We call it a city, not a village. It looks nothing like this. Our buildings are tall with bright lights. And there are many more people than here."

They walked in silence for a few moments, and

Zwaantie reflected on how different this felt. She had never taken the time to get to know any of the other princes. She didn't want to. A breeze blew, and Zwaantie noticed that Leo's hair didn't move. It was so strange, spiky like that.

"Tell me more about this prince that you're going to marry," he said.

"I haven't decided who I'm going to marry yet. Honesty, I'd rather not marry at all. I keep telling Mother that, but she doesn't listen."

But you will marry. Soon.

Zwaantie paused. She almost told him that she didn't want to be queen, but she wasn't about to say that again for fear of what would happen. The Voice was in her head again, after the wall, like normal. For some reason that brought a strange comfort to her. She wasn't sure she'd like it if the Voice disappeared altogether. Even if she was afraid it was trying to kill her.

She glanced over at Leo, surprised at how comfortable she was talking to him. Perhaps it was because he was temporary. Someone who would disappear in two weeks and take her secrets with him.

"I want to marry for love. The princes are not looking for love. They are looking for a princess. They don't see me. And not one of them has ever even been interested in me for a moment. Including you. You pranced into our palace and announced your intentions without even so much as a glance in my direction."

"What was I supposed to do? Announce that I just wanted to visit Sol and get to know the royal family? They would've been highly suspicious."

"I suppose you have a point, but don't you think the whole process feels so wrong? I mean, what if you totally hated me, or suppose I was ugly and fat. Would you still marry me then?"

"I'm doing what is best for my country. If that means being unhappy with my wife, then I will do that."

Zwaantie didn't know how to react to that. He was braver than her for sure. She couldn't imagine giving up her happiness up for the sake of her country. She felt a little embarrassed of herself.

"Well, we've already established that I will not marry you. So you are off the hook."

"Forgive me for being bold, but I haven't given up yet. You are most beautiful and charming. I think I would be happy with you. Is there any way I can convince you to reconsider?"

Oh, he was good. Complimenting her like that and then trying to see what he could do to win her over. Zwaantie did not like where this conversation was going. Time to pull out the real charm.

"Well, the last suitor refused to moo for me. I will definitely not marry someone who won't moo for me."

He looked puzzled. "What is mooing?"

Zwaantie stopped, right in the middle of the street. "Mooing, you know, like a cow."

"What's a cow?"

"A farm animal. Cows, chickens, sheep, goats, pigs, horses."

Leo furrowed his brow. "I've heard of horses and chickens, but none of the others."

"Have you ever eaten beef?" Zwaantie was dumbfounded. Their whole world revolved around those animals. How could he not know?

"Of course. It comes from here. We can't grow our own food, and animals are hard to keep without fields."

"Where did you think beef came from?"

He shrugged. "Never thought of it much."

The village was the wrong place to be. They needed to visit the farm. The royal farm was smaller than most of the outlying farms, but they still had all the required animals. As a child, Zwaantie's favorite thing to do was milk cows and collect eggs. Which Mother put a stop to the day she got her monthlies. After that she had to be a real princess who sewed and visited with other princesses.

"Let's go visit a farm. Though, you'll need to change your clothes."

"Why?" He looked down at his fluffy white shirt, poofy pants, vest, and flimsy shoes.

"Look at those shoes. They don't protect your feet at all."

"These are sandals. What do my feet need protecting from anyway?"

"Dirt, rocks, cow poop. I need to change too."

He pointed at her feet. "Okay, but I am not wearing shoes like that."

"Fine, but you can't wear those either. And don't get mad if you mess up your pretty leather boots."

"Where are you taking me, the swamp?"

"Something like that, but more fun. Let's go change."

Zwaantie was a little excited to show him her world. Plus, he was easier to talk to than she had planned. Maybe it was because he was from Stella. She'd always felt more comfortable with Luna and Phoenix than she ever had with any of her royal friends.

Zwaantie hurried to her room. As she rounded the corner, she ran right into Phoenix. He grinned as he helped steady her. Pieter was with him, and Luna stood on her tiptoes and gave him a kiss.

"Aw, aren't you two cute?" Zwaantie asked, still not letting go of Phoenix. She liked standing there, practically in his arms.

Luna blushed. "Well, the Voice doesn't care anymore if we kiss."

Zwaantie met Phoenix's eyes. "Must be nice."

His gaze burned into hers. She was so very close. A few inches and she'd get a kiss of her own.

Phoenix let go of her and took two steps back. She couldn't help her disappointment.

"Where are you going in such a hurry?" he asked.

"The prince has never seen a farm, so we're going to show him around. I didn't want to get my yellow dress dirty."

Phoenix raised his eyebrows. "Do you like the Stellan prince?"

Zwaantie shrugged. "He's just like any of the others. Boring."

Phoenix gave a sharp nod. "Well, we need to head on. Raaf and the king sent us to fetch the new weapons. They want to play with them."

As they walked away, Zwaantie had a sinking feeling. Someone was trying to kill her. It'd be a lot easier with those new weapons.

Chapter 19

The Cow: Part 2

Leo wrinkled his nose. "What are those things?"

The pigs rolled around in the muck and snorted. Zwaantie loved the farm. If she hadn't chosen midwifery for her contribution, she would've picked something related to farming. Somehow, she didn't think Mother would let her be a farmer even if she'd tried.

"Pigs. We get bacon and pork from them."

He breathed out. "Bacon smells a hellava lot better than that."

"Yes, well, we wash them first," Zwaantie said without cracking a smile.

"With what?" he asked with a frown.

"Soap."

Leo looked at her and smiled. "Bacon doesn't smell like soap either. And I've butchered fish before, so I imagine pigs are the same way. Good thing we don't eat the outside of them, huh?"

So, he wasn't dumb. That was good to know.

He backed away from the pigpen, and Zwaantie followed. She couldn't tell what he was thinking. She wanted him to like the farm, and it bothered her that she wanted his approval. She wasn't sure what she thought of him, but he had to get off the marriage idea.

"Come on." She waved him to the chicken coop. "The chickens aren't quite so stinky. Would you like to gather some eggs with me?"

"Sure. My mother cooked for fun, and she taught me her tricks. She used to create mountains of scrambled eggs for me in rainbow colors. I was twelve before I knew that the natural color for eggs was yellow."

Part of Zwaantie yearned to understand that magic, but part of her was repulsed by changing food with magic.

A slave handed them baskets, and they set about finding eggs. She stuck her hand in a box and withdrew an egg. Leo watched her for a few moments.

He stuck his hand in another box without looking. Maybe he wasn't so smart.

"Yow," he yelled and jerked his hand out.

Zwaantie looked down and saw an angry red mark on his hand. Then she giggled. A hen stuck her head out of the opening of the box and clucked at him.

"You are supposed to check the box before you

stick your hand inside. She thinks you are taking her babies." Zwaantie laughed again. He scowled for a second and then smiled at her.

"Can we cook these when we get back to the castle?"

"The slaves will do it. Though I doubt they know how to make it pretty colors."

"You never do any of your own cooking?" he asked, checking another box before sticking his hand in and pulling out a small brown egg.

Zwaantie watched him. "A few royals do. The ones who decide to make it their hobby. I chose midwifery, so I've never cooked anything."

"Ah, Princess, you are missing out. When you come to Stella with me, I will teach you how to cook."

Oh, he had some nerve. She frowned at him. "What makes you think I'm coming to Stella with you?"

His smile faltered, and he blushed. Good. He was too sure of himself.

"I'm sorry. I got carried away. I really like you. I mean, I know I just met you, but you are truly the most beautiful girl I've ever seen."

Now it was Zwaantie's turn to blush. Her stomach buzzed, but it also made her nervous. She was in love with Phoenix. Guilt gnawed at her insides. Her stomach shouldn't be fluttering for anyone else.

Leo glanced over to Hunter and Luna. They seemed to be enjoying a lively conversation. At least they were getting along.

"Come, I want to introduce you to the sheep." She handed off the eggs to a couple of slaves, and Leo strolled next to her through the field.

"Why do your people wear bondage bands?" he asked.

"They are slaves."

"I don't understand. The only people who wear them in our kingdom are prisoners. And they wear them only so that we can know to not trust them. But you have so many. Even your maid wears them."

"She is a slave. Her mother chose to become a slave."

He stepped around a sheep and wrinkled his brow. "What is a slave, exactly?"

"When our people cannot feed themselves, they choose to become slaves. They agree to serve in whatever capacity the city needs in exchange for food, shelter, and basic clothing. The bondage bands are placed to make sure they follow the agreement. It lasts one hundred years for themselves and any posterity they have. After a hundred years, the bands fall off."

"How is that fair?" he asked, his frown deepening.

"They do work hard for what they are given, so it

is fair to the kingdom." She'd been questioning some of the slave practices recently, but the system was efficient, and while it wasn't the best for some individuals, the overall practice was necessary.

His face went beet red, and he stopped abruptly. Hunter came running. "Your Highness, is something wrong?"

"I'm fine. But there is something seriously twisted here."

Leo grabbed Luna's arm and shook her band in Zwaantie's face. "Your slave didn't choose this life. Her mother did. How is it fair to her that she should have to live like this? And her children and grandchildren? This is a sick system."

Zwaantie squared her shoulders and raised her head. "They live good lives. At least ours do. If we didn't have the system in place, they would starve." This was her home, and she wasn't about to let a snotty prince from Stella tell her how to run her kingdom.

Leo stalked off across the field toward the castle. Zwaantie followed but didn't get the chance to warn him before he stepped in a pile of cow poop.

"Oh, for the love of all the stars!" he yelled and held his foot up. "What is this?" he asked, pointing to the steaming crap with a wrinkled nose.

She giggled. "Cow poop."

He muttered under his breath and wiped his foot on the grass. He held onto a tree to steady himself.

"Why do you like it out here?" he asked as she drew nearer to him.

"I told you. The cows."

"I still have no idea what a cow is."

Zwaantie smirked as a cow walked up behind him and bellowed in his ear. He jumped and stormed away. Zwaantie, Luna, and even Hunter laughed.

Leo was sulky and silent all the way to the palace. Just before they got to the entrance, he stopped Zwaantie.

"I'm sorry. We don't have slaves in Stella, and the idea just seems so horrific to me. And then I stepped in, well, you know. Forgive me?"

She shook her head. "No, you ruined my afternoon. But if you do something for me, I will." She was wicked, but she couldn't help herself.

"Whatever you want." He said and bowed extravagantly, a crooked smile on his face.

"Moo for me."

Luna giggled behind her.

Leo's face was impassive. She had no idea what he would do. But without warning, he let out a huge bellow and grinned at her.

"Thank you," she said, genuinely pleased.

"I'll see you at dinner," he said. Then he leaned

over and kissed her on the cheek.

He and Hunter sauntered into the castle. Luna's face had gone pale. Zwaantie had just been kissed for the first time in her life by someone other than her parents.

And it wasn't Phoenix.

The Voice immediately began its assault.

You filthy girl. How dare you let him do that to you? You should go scrub your face with acid to burn off the filth. Filthy, filthy girl.

Chapter 20

The Kiss

Zwaantie didn't go into the castle. She marched away and down the street. She ignored the slaves and merchants who fell to the ground in a bow.

Filthy girl. A small headache formed between her eyes, but it wasn't bad. The Voice continued to call her all sorts of names.

She stomped inside Wilma's cottage. Wilma looked up from a book she was reading. "Goodness sakes, child, why are you making such a racket?"

"That prince," she fumed. She paced in front of Wilma.

Wilma closed her book, took off her reading glasses, and watched Zwaantie. "What did he do?"

"He kissed me," she spat.

Wilma laughed. "I'd take a kiss from him any day."

Zwaantie glared at her. "Well, you can have him. I hope the Voice is yelling at you, by the way. This isn't funny."

"Honey, he's a doll and probably your future husband. What's wrong with him kissing you?"

Zwaantie stopped and shook her finger in Wilma's

face. "Take that back. He will not be my husband. I don't love him. And he's from Stella. How dare you even suggest it."

"Most marriages aren't for love. He's a good choice, better than any of the Solite princes."

"He's from Stella." Zwaantie couldn't believe Wilma was actually suggesting she marry the prince. Sure, Zwaantie enjoyed the magic from Stella, but they were too different. Their culture of touching and kissing and obscene clothes.

"So?"

"So, they're…they're barbarians. He kissed me!"

Wilma stood and pointed at the table. "Let me make you a cup of tea and help you calm down."

"I don't want to calm down."

Wilma bustled about making tea. Zwaantie sat at the table fuming. Not only was Wilma unsympathetic, but she actually thought Zwaantie should marry that creep. At least the Voice stopped berating her. Maybe it realized the kiss wasn't her fault.

Wilma brought two steaming cups to the table.

"When is the wedding?" Wilma asked with a grin.

Zwaantie glared at her and sipped her tea. It burned going down, but Wilma's teas were the best. This tasted of lavender and vanilla.

Wilma was altogether too eager to see her marry

Leo. Time to change the subject.

"Did you hear about my guard?"

Wilma sat across from her. "The one who jumped off the bridge? Yes. I did."

"And did you know how that girl died the other night at dinner? Was it possible she was poisoned?"

Wilma shrugged. "Maybe. Why?"

Zwaantie hadn't wanted to admit this out loud. But she was starting to see patterns. "I think someone is trying to kill me. Or rather. I think the Voice is."

Wilma took a sip of her tea and stared into her cup. "Why would you think that?"

"Because I told Mother that I didn't want to be queen. She said Sol wouldn't let me abdicate. What if this is Sol's way of making sure I don't?"

Wilma raised her eyebrows. "By killing you?"

"It sounds stupid, I know. But that girl died, my guard tried to kill me, and the Voice tried to lure me into the wall."

"I checked the girl out, and it did not look like poison to me. Though I will admit poison can be hard to detect. The wall though, you didn't tell me about that."

Zwaantie explained how the Voice tried to make her step into the wall.

"Now, that's easy. You were too close to the wall.

That wasn't the Voice at all, but the wall trying to trick you. As for your guard. Obviously, he was going mad. Otherwise, he wouldn't have taken his own life. Does that ease your fears?"

Zwaantie nodded, but she still felt uneasy about the whole thing. Something was off.

Wilma looked out the window to the sun. "You must go. I don't think your mother will let you miss another dinner."

The slave chefs created quite the feast for the prince. Everything was super fresh, from the greens to the sausages. The prince seemed so in love with the food Zwaantie was surprised he even had time to carry on a conversation with Raaf.

Zwaantie wasn't speaking to Leo, which he took in stride, but she listened to his conversation with Raaf.

"Do you have many siblings?" Raaf asked.

"Yes. I only have one full sister. But through my father I have ten additional siblings. My mother also has three more sons, but I don't see them much."

Zwaantie didn't understand. She wanted to ask, but didn't want to talk to him. Having siblings without the same parents seemed so foreign. It happened occasionally when someone died, but he had half siblings from both parents.

"What do you mean?" Raaf asked. "Does your father have more than one wife?"

"Oh no. My mother and father never married. My mother married her current husband after she had me."

Raaf seemed speechless. "Do you plan on having children before you are married?"

"Of course not. Only the king does that. Well, officially anyway. Several of my siblings are already married. One of my brothers on my mother's side married a Solite, actually."

Zwaantie nearly broke her vow of silence, but Raaf beat her to it.

"How is that possible? Solites are not allowed to cross the wall."

"I don't know. Like I said, I'm not close to that brother. He lives in a different city. But he brought his wife to the castle to have my father remove her bondage bands. I thought she must've been a prisoner. But now I understand she was a slave."

Raaf went quiet, and Zwaantie cursed him. She wanted to hear more. But then Raaf changed the subject and waxed on about Sol's discipline system, which seemed to fascinate Leo but bored Zwaantie to tears.

The strawberry shortcake arrived, and Zwaantie was grateful dinner was almost over.

"This is amazing. I've never had strawberries that taste like this. How do you do it?" Leo asked her.

A direct question. She wasn't sure she could ignore that. Zwaantie pointed up. "The sun."

He nodded. "So why are you mad at me? I've been trying to figure it out, but I'm lost. I mooed for you."

"You kissed me." She shuddered at the thought.

A crease appeared in his forehead.

"I did?"

"Yes, on the cheek. No one has ever kissed me before."

"That was highly inappropriate," Raaf said. "Didn't the Voice warn you?"

Zwaantie glared at her brother. "No, it didn't warn me. I didn't know he was going to do it. But the guilt was horrid."

Raaf speared one of his strawberries. "I wasn't talking to you. I was talking to Leo," Raaf said.

"No, the Voice didn't warn me. Why would it?" Leo scratched his forehead.

"If the Voice can tell what you are about to do something wrong, it will warn you so you don't do it. Surely it could tell what you were doing."

"I'm sorry. The Voice said nothing to me." He faced Zwaantie. "What did the Voice say after I kissed you?"

She blushed. "I don't want to tell you, but it made

me feel bad about the kiss, and it's your fault."

Leo picked up his fork again. "It was a simple kiss on the cheek. I often give my sisters the same. I'm sorry if I offended you, but in Stella, kissing on the cheek is considered a polite form of greeting. Probably why the Voice didn't warn me. It's not wrong for me."

Raaf frowned. "That's interesting. The ways of the Voice are mysterious. I wonder what else you can do that we cannot because it is not forbidden in Stella."

Leo shrugged. "You must teach me how to get food like this in Stella. We try with magic, but it doesn't even compare."

After dinner, Zwaantie escaped out to the rock where she and Phoenix met. She needed to think. Phoenix wouldn't be there for an hour at least, and she wanted to be alone. Voices came from the other side of the hedge. Zwaantie listened for a moment. It was Leo and his guard. She crept toward the hedge.

"She is gorgeous. This is bloody awful," Leo said. Zwaantie's stomach buzzed again. She shouldn't react to the fact that he thought she was beautiful. She loved Phoenix.

"How is that a bad thing?" Hunter asked.

"She's funny and beautiful. What do I have to offer her that no other suitor has? Especially since her father has no interest in entertaining the thought."

"You are a high prince. From Stella, which is a hellava lot better than here. And no offense, she's pretty and all, but not gorgeous."

"You're just saying that because you are over the moon in love with Candace. If you weren't, you'd agree with me."

Zwaantie crouched down so she could see them. They sat with their backs to a tree. Hunter pulled an apple out of his bag. "Speaking of Candace, do you remember that she promised to castrate you if you didn't have me back in time for the baby? So whatever you need to do, do it quick." He took a big bite of the apple. "Stars, the fruit here is amazing."

"Father will kill me if I don't return with her. But I made a complete ass of myself today."

"Yeah, you sort of did. The cow dung didn't help. At least it doesn't smell as bad as dog poop."

The prince smiled. "I miss Molly. Have you noticed they have no pets here? No cats, dogs, or birds. Just cows and pigs and crap."

Hunter shrugged. "Maybe we can bring her a kitten or something. That might work. We'd have to go back home first though."

Leo grimaced. "That will take too long."

"Focus. We aren't going anywhere until you get the princess to marry you. What are you going to do?"

"I don't know. This shouldn't be that hard."

Hunter shook his head and swallowed. "You are a prince. Woo her. Don't they teach you that in prince school?"

Leo slugged Hunter in the arm. "I have an idea. Let's go talk to her servants and find out what she does when she thinks no one is looking. I'll find a way to win to her heart."

They ran to the castle, and Zwaantie rocked back on her heels. Leo wasn't interested in any trade agreements. He wanted one thing and one thing only.

Her.

The question was why. He'd given no good reason, but he said his father would kill him if he didn't marry her. What was so special about her?

The problem with Leo was that he was incredibly charming. If he convinced Father and Mother that he was a good match, Zwaantie might not have a choice.

She had to figure out how to get out of this. Because unless she was walking down the aisle with Phoenix, she didn't want to do it all.

Chapter 21

The Declaration

Phoenix joined her on the rock an hour later. "Missed you last night," he said.

"I know. I had to help deliver babies. I didn't get home till nearly gray. Besides, Luna said you were with Raaf anyway."

"I got here late and just assumed you didn't wait for me."

They sat in silence for a few moments. Then Phoenix spoke. His voice was low and quiet. "I saw the prince kiss you outside the castle. Did you agree to marry him?"

Zwaantie's chest burned. "No. I didn't ask for any of that. I'm not going to marry him." She took his hand. "I love you more than anything. I'm going to marry you. I don't know how or what it will take, but I will."

The Voice went bananas. *Take that back. Foul girl. You know your place.*

A pinch started in her forehead. But her declaration was worth the pain. Zwaantie figured while she was at it, she might as well give the Voice something to really berate her for. That cow-hole Leo had already kissed her cheek, and she was going to be damn sure he didn't get one on her lips before Phoenix did.

She hopped off the rock and motioned for him to join her. He landed right next to her. "Who's chasing who?" he asked.

"No one."

She grabbed both of his hands and wove their fingers together. He smiled at her, and she took a step closer. So far, the Voice didn't seem to notice anything out of the ordinary. Zwaantie met his smoldering eyes. She should've kissed him when he was in her room. She was done waiting.

She stood on her tiptoes and pressed her mouth against his. His lips were soft against hers, but he didn't react. Just stood there still as a maple tree. Zwaantie pulled away, her chest tight.

"I'm sorry," he said with sad eyes. "I couldn't do it. I love you though."

Filthy, filthy girl.

A blinding pain overtook her forehead, and she knew that for the first time in her life, she would have to confess to her brother.

Chapter 22

The Failure

The Voice called over Zwaantie's orb and removed the guilt. He thought about just letting her suffer and maybe allowing that to drive her mad. In the end though, he was afraid that would lead to questions about him. A peasant or slave with unending pain was one thing. The princess was quite another.

A clatter sounded behind him. Oh Sol, she was back again.

He spun around.

"She's onto you," the woman said.

"Excuse me?"

"Zwaantie. She knows it is the Voice."

"How would you know that?"

"I overheard a conversation between her and one of her friends. She knows. Need I remind you what happens if you don't stop this? The prince from Stella plans on winning her heart. I daresay he's almost succeeded."

The Voice laughed. "No. He's not. Trust me."

"Regardless. She suspects you. What are you going to do about that?"

"Does it matter if she suspects me or not? I got close last time."

"With the guard?"

"No. The wall. Though the guard was a near miss. If Zwaantie had come home even ten minutes earlier, he would've killed her, but she was too close to midnight, and my influence ended before he had a chance to finish. The next one will work."

"And what, pray tell, is the next one?"

"None of your business." This woman had done nothing so far to help him. He wasn't about to reveal his plans to her.

"It is my business. I need her dead as much as you do."

"Trust me. She doesn't have a single person dear to her who won't attempt to kill her before this is all over. The whispers are planting seeds."

The woman pounded her fist on the table. "You cannot fail. If she even gets close to crossing the Stellan border, I will intervene, and you won't like my methods."

Then she turned on the spot and disappeared.

Chapter 23

The Snoop

The next morning, Mother summoned Zwaantie to her room. She probably just wanted an update on how things were going with Leo. Zwaantie could report that she'd been a good girl. Usually Luna would accompany her when she visited her mother, but she'd sent Luna off to find out if Wilma would need her later. She was looking for an excuse to not have to be with Leo.

She knocked, and Ariel peeked out.

"My mother sent for me."

"Yes, come in." Ariel opened the door wider, and Zwaantie swept into the room. She saw Raaf sitting in another chair, Phoenix standing behind him.

She didn't look at Phoenix as she approached the chairs. She was afraid her face would betray her.

She took her seat carefully and smiled. "How are you, Mother?"

Mother scowled at her. "Tell me, Zwaantie, are you in love?"

"Of course not. Who would I possibly be in love with?" Zwaantie hoped against hope that this wasn't the moment where Mother decided she marry Leo.

Mother shook her head. "I was taking a stroll in my garden yesterday, and it was stuffy and crowded and I wanted to be alone so I wandered a little to the west. To my surprise I overheard the most interesting conversation."

Zwaantie paled. She tried to keep her expression neutral.

"Oh, and what did you hear?"

"My daughter, the crown princess, swearing her undying love for a slave. She even promised to marry him. Can you imagine how shocked I was to hear such a conversation?"

Phoenix squeezed his eyes shut.

"Mother, I can explain."

Mother narrowed her eyes. "No. You cannot. I understand now our previous conversations. I have given you options, Zwaantie. I have been nice about this, but no more. You have been shirking your responsibility, and it's time for you to step up and take your place. Maybe then you'll stop with these foolish notions. Once all of the princes arrive, you will have three days to pick one, or I will see to it that Phoenix is executed for his crimes. Do you understand?"

Zwaantie's chest tightened, and her palms began to sweat. Phoenix had done nothing wrong. What was mother thinking? "What crimes?" she asked with desperation.

"Persuading the princess to love him. For a slave, that is death."

"You wouldn't." Zwaantie squeezed her eyes shut. She'd never thought that far. How stupid of her to not think of Phoenix's life.

"I would."

"Mother, I must protest," Raaf spoke up. Oh, thank the stars, Raaf would save her.

"Excuse me, Raaf, but what does this have to do with you?"

"Phoenix is my slave. I need him. You can't take him away from me."

Mother narrowed her eyes at Phoenix. "What is this sorcery you have done? Have you bewitched both of my children? I cannot believe I allowed you to play with them. That was my mistake. I won't make it again. For now, you will work with the sewage slaves. Zwaantie obviously needs some persuading. But if she doesn't marry a prince, you will see your death. I promise you that. Guards, bring him to the sewers."

Tears fell freely. Zwaantie watched as they dragged him away. Her heart shattered. She wanted to save him, but she couldn't. She tried to hold in the sobs, but they came anyway.

"Now, go to your room. I will summon all of the lower princes to the castle and you will announce your engagement within the month."

Chapter 24

The Revelation

Zwaantie spent most of the next day crying in her bed. Luna bustled around the room but didn't try to talk to her. She must be upset as well, but all Zwaantie could focus on was the pain in her stomach. Not only had she lost the love of her life, she was now going to be forced to marry someone else. And poor Phoenix. He was in the sewers, shoveling out the muck and refuse. This was her fault.

Sometime after lunch, Luna flung the covers off.

"Get up. I know you are upset, but at this point, our goal is keep Phoenix alive. To do that, you must choose a husband. You need to go for a walk, clear your head, and be ready to charm the ones who've arrived at dinner."

Zwaantie wanted to hit her. "Who is here?"

"Vache. I heard Ryker will make it before dinner because he was already in town visiting with the lower king and queen of Zonnes. It will take Willem and Isaac a few more days."

Oh Sol, they were already here. Luna was right.

Zwaantie had to keep Phoenix alive.

"Okay," Zwaantie said and swung her legs out of bed.

"You need to change first and let me fix your hair. Then, while you are out, I'll clean up this room."

Zwaantie changed and washed her face. After Luna did her hair, she went out to the garden. Phoenix wouldn't be there, but she just wanted to be in a place where they'd been happy.

Just as she started down the path to the pond, a hand gripped her elbow. She spun around.

"Leo, what are you doing here?"

"Taking a walk."

"Where is Hunter?"

"He's training with a few of your guards. I was bored, so I thought I'd check out the gardens. Would you like to join me?"

She wanted to say no, but she couldn't. She took a deep breath, let it out, and tucked her arm into his elbow. The wandered toward the roses. She did not want to talk about herself, so she quickly asked him a question. "What's your family like?"

"Loud."

"You can give me more than that."

"Father's a typical king. Though he spends more time with me than yours does with you, I think."

"That wouldn't be hard. I don't see my father

often. What do you do with him?"

"He likes to take me out among the people. We'll go to a bar or restaurant and mingle. Father taught me how to gauge the happiness of our people by how they behave around us."

"Why? You aren't heir to the throne."

He pursed his lips. "No, I'm not. Nevertheless, my father thought it was best to teach me how to handle the affairs of the kingdom. I will likely be a close advisor when my brother becomes king."

A tickle of memory came to Zwaantie. The last time Leo spoke of his father, he mentioned how his father had removed bondage bands.

"Didn't you say you had a brother who was married to Solite slave?"

"Yes."

"Can your father remove all bondage bands?" Perhaps she could somehow find a way to sneak Phoenix across the border. If that Solite woman did it, then it must be possible. But Zwaantie didn't want to be too hopeful. Not yet.

"Of course. So can I."

Zwaantie's heart stilled. She kept her voice steady as she tried to make sense of things. "Can all Stellans remove them?"

"No. Only a few. I can do it because I deal with prisoners sometimes."

"I thought you said you were an academic mage."

He gave her a wink. "I lied. Sort of."

"What's that supposed to mean?"

"Well, I am an academic mage, but I don't sit around reading books all day."

"What do you do?"

"I work closely with our head mage. She's similar in rank to your brother."

Zwaantie wanted to ask more, but the wheels in her head were spinning. This changed everything. Mother had not been specific enough. She said pick a prince. She didn't say she couldn't marry the Stellan.

Chapter 25

The Announcement

The next morning Zwaantie woke early, buzzing with excitement about her plan. She spent all night planning how she would pull this off. She'd nearly told the prince she would marry him last night but figured that would be too suspicious. This would be epic.

Luna arrived after Zwaantie awoke. She seemed harried and worried.

"I want my best dress," Zwaantie said.

"Well, you're just going to have to wait," Luna snapped.

Whoa.

"What's the matter?" Zwaantie asked.

Luna shook her head. "I don't feel good. Sorry."

Zwaantie smiled. Luna's foul mood couldn't ruin hers.

"What color dress?"

"The green," Zwaantie replied.

She hauled out the dress and then scowled at Zwaantie. "Why are you in such a good mood? Or have you forgotten about my brother?"

Zwaantie felt as if she'd been slapped. "No. Of course not. I have a plan. I found out yesterday that Leo can remove bondage bands in Stella. So I'm going to tell him I'll marry him and then make sure he takes Phoenix with us. Then Phoenix and I will run away in Stella." Zwaantie bounced on the bed. She was pretty pleased with herself.

Luna blinked for a second. "It's a stupid plan."

"What's stupid about it?" Zwaantie was hurt.

"Where are you going to live? Work? You've never worked a day in your life. Do you think you can live like normal people do? Because that's what you'll have to do. And don't think you'll be able to come back to Sol. Your father will have people looking everywhere for you, and then they'll execute the both of you."

She made it seem like Zwaantie hadn't thought about that. Which she hadn't, but that was beside the point.

"I'll just get work as a midwife in Stella. They have babies there too."

Luna slipped the dress over Zwaantie's head. "They have mages who deliver babies. They won't need a midwife."

Zwaantie hadn't thought of that. She could learn. Maybe magic was teachable. Plus, Phoenix was employable.

"We'll figure it out."

"Still stupid. But you never did listen to me anyway. Come on, let's go ruin your life."

Zwaantie paused for a second. "Wait. Something is wrong. Tell me."

Luna rubbed her forehead. "No, it's not. I don't feel good, but I still have to work. I know you're excited about this plan, but all I can see is how many ways in which it can go wrong."

"Say the word, and I won't do it."

Luna gave her a sad smile. "I'm not about to tell the future queen what to do. I think it's stupid, but I'll still support you in your decision."

The prince's room was three doors down from hers. This early in the morning the hallways were empty. Luna knocked, and Zwaantie waited. Hunter opened the door, his hair disheveled. He wore only a pair of short shorts. Zwaantie looked away quickly and felt bad for Luna. She had to look at him.

Luna coughed. "The princess would like to speak to High Prince Leo."

"Of course," he said, "One moment, please."

They heard bumps and bangs from the other side, and two minutes later the door opened. Hunter had managed to put some pants on but nothing else. His chest was distracting.

"Ladies, come in." He gestured into the room.

Luna followed after Zwaantie. Leo stood near the fireplace, dressed as he had yesterday before they went to see the cows. He bowed when he saw her.

"Luna, Hunter, I would like to speak with the prince alone. Will you excuse us?"

Luna hurried out of the room, but Hunter hesitated. He walked over to the prince and whispered something in his ear. The prince nodded and then dismissed him with a wave. He left and looked back just before he shut the door behind him.

"Would you like to sit, Princess?" Leo asked.

He seemed nervous, unsure of himself.

She sat and stared at him for a moment. She took a deep breath. There were a thousand ways this could go wrong, but she had to try. This was the only way she could save Phoenix.

"If I were to marry you, how would that work? Where would we live? What about the wedding? Do you have anything you want from us?"

He seemed taken aback by the question. "I thought that you didn't want to marry me."

Zwaantie fiddled with the lace on her dress and looked down, demure. "Just curious."

"Curious enough to wake me up?"

She shrugged and waited.

"Well, we would live here, obviously. I'm the fifth son. I have no kingdom in Stella. And you are the crown princess. My only request is that we get married in Stella because my father won't risk a visit to Sol. After that, we would need to visit our outlying kingdoms so the rest of the citizens of Stella could meet you. It is customary when a prince or princess gets married. It would take about a year. Then we would come back here, because you are the crown princess. As for me wanting anything, your hand is all I've ever wanted since I've laid eyes on you." The prince pushed his feet against the footrest, which caused the chair to rock back and forth on two legs.

Zwaantie blushed and stared at him from under her eyelashes.

"Sounds reasonable enough. I will marry you."

He toppled over backwards. Zwaantie laughed, and he scrambled up. He picked up the chair and sat down, his face red.

"Ha ha, nice joke," he said.

"I'm not joking."

"Right, ever since I've gotten here, you've done nothing but laugh at me. And scowl occasionally. Besides, you told me that you weren't interested in marrying."

"I wasn't. But I changed my mind."

"Right. And what exactly changed your mind?"

"You make me laugh."

He grinned a little. "Okay, you've had your fun. But

I must get myself ready for breakfast. As much as you like to laugh at me, your parents don't, and I need to make myself presentable."

Zwaantie sighed. He still didn't believe her. "Before we announce our plans to my parents, I have a request."

"What plans?" he asked.

"To get married."

He rolled his eyes. "I don't think your parents will appreciate the joke."

"No, they wouldn't if I was joking, but I'm not. I need you to ask them for something. It is customary for the king to offer the groom a gift of his choosing, and I'm asking you to ask for a gift for me, since you said you didn't want anything."

He sank into his chair. "Holy stars, you are serious."

"Yes, I am. Now will you do that for me? Ask them for something for me, but you can't tell them it's for me. You have to pretend you want it."

He squeezed his eyes shut and then opened them again. "Okay, you mean it. You want to marry me."

"Yeah. I do."

"Fine, I'll play along. But if this is some sick joke to anger your parents, I'll never forgive you. And you don't want a high prince of Stella as your enemy."

He stood and paced back and forth in front of the

fireplace. He was handsome. Someday he would make his wife happy. But that girl would not be Zwaantie. She almost felt bad for what she was about to do.

"I'm not playing. A year away from home is a long time. I want to bring along Luna. But she won't leave without her brother and husband. So you need to ask for your choice of any three slaves in the kingdom."

His eyes darkened, and his voice grew cold. "We don't have slaves in Stella, and I won't bring any there. You ask for too much, Princess."

"Well, they wouldn't have to be slaves in Stella. The Voice doesn't work over there, right?"

He rubbed his hand over his face. "If I bring them over, I'm removing those bondage bands. They won't be slaves when we come back here."

"That's fine."

"Then I'm not asking for just three then. If we are going to release them, I want to bring more. How many could I ask for without angering your father?"

Now it was Zwaantie's turn to be surprised. "I don't know. We should just stick to the three. I don't think I'm worth more than that."

"You are worth far more than that." He got up and kissed her cheek. "Now, I do need to get ready. We'll announce our engagement at breakfast. Shall I fetch you from your room in twenty minutes?"

Zwaantie nodded, a bit unsure of what she'd just done. She hoped he wouldn't ruin it with his grand plans.

They entered the room together, Zwaantie's arm tucked in his elbow. Mother raised her eyebrows but didn't say anything. Zwaantie tried her best not to act nervous or upset, but until she knew for sure that Phoenix would accompany her, she didn't want to get too excited. Plus, there's the I'm-about-to-announce-a-marriage-to-a-man-I-don't-want-to-marry thing. It didn't matter that Zwaantie knew she wasn't going to marry him. She was still worried about the whole thing.

As soon as they finished eating, Leo took her hand, and they stood in front of her parents. Breakfast had been odd and awkward. She was tense, but Leo was all smiles.

They both bowed. Mother pursed her lips. Zwaantie had surprised her many times by making brash announcements or asking for things she shouldn't. The Voice never warned her against those things. Sometimes, she almost wished the Voice could read her thoughts.

Leo spoke. "As you know, my purpose in coming to Sol was to secure the hand of your daughter in marriage. This morning, she and I discussed the idea at length, and she has agreed to marry me."

At that moment, Zwaantie should have looked at Leo and smiled. Instead, Zwaantie stared at the ground, thinking of Phoenix.

"No," Mother gasped.

Father cleared his throat. "I thought we made it clear that Zwaantie will marry a Solite prince."

"You did. Zwaantie explained to me that who she marries is her own choice. She chose me. She assured me you would be supportive."

Zwaantie met her mother's eyes with defiance. She'd said pick a prince. She didn't say he couldn't be from Stella.

Mother held her gaze for a few moments. "Very well, then we shall begin wedding plans immediately." Mother never lost her composure for long. She knew Zwaantie was only doing this to get back at her, and she would make sure Zwaantie felt the full impact of her choice.

"I'm sorry to disappoint the high queen, but Zwaantie has agreed to get married in Stella so that my father can attend. We would love to have you travel to our kingdom and be present for the wedding. It will take place in three months' time."

Mother scowled, but recovered quickly and smiled. "Before you leave, we must have the traditional wedding ball. We hardly ever get the excuse to have a dance, and I want to use this one.

We can have it ready in four days."

Zwaantie gave her a tight smile.

Father had been suspiciously quiet. Zwaantie looked to him. His face was impassive.

"It is customary when a groom chooses a bride to ask the father for anything under his jurisdiction. As high king, all of Sol falls under mine. What is it you would ask for your gift?"

"I would like my choice of fifty of your slaves."

Zwaantie staggered for a moment. "Three," she whispered furiously to him. "I told you three."

He brought his lips close to her ears. "And I told you that you were worth more than that. I almost asked for a hundred."

Father's eyes burned with anger. This would all fall apart. "Perhaps you do not understand how the slave system works. They take care of our city. Keep it free of trash and debris. They also take care of us. Fifty is an awful lot of slaves that we would have to replace. You may have five."

"Do you not think your daughter is worth fifty slaves?"

Father bristled. "Of course she is. But what do you need fifty slaves for?"

"We do not have slaves in Stella. I find I have enjoyed being taken care of. Plus, we could use some cleaning of our streets as well. And your daughter will be gone for nearly a year. Surely she needs slaves to take care of her. But if you do not agree to fifty, then seventy-five will do."

Father stood, his face flushing. "No, absolutely not."

"Then we do not have an agreement." Leo bowed quickly to Zwaantie and stalked from the room, Hunter close on his heels.

Zwaantie raced after them, not even looking up at her parents. They were halfway down the hall to Leo's room when she caught him. She jerked him around and slapped him across the face. "What the darkness were you thinking? I thought you wanted to marry me. Not to mention that my father is a high king. What right did you have to speak to him that way? You're lucky he agreed to the marriage at all. Now you've ruined it. He'll never agree to the marriage."

You should not strike another. A pain flashed behind her eyes, but it quickly disappeared.

He brought his hand to his face, but grinned. "I didn't realize you were so eager to marry me."

"Of course I am. But now you've ruined it."

He grasped her hands and stared down at her with those deep brown eyes. "No, I haven't. Your father will come around."

"He won't come around. You've just made him

angry."

"I'll visit with him this afternoon. I promise by tonight, we'll have an agreement. I've done my fair share of negotiating with difficult people. This will not be hard."

He didn't understand Zwaantie's father. No way would he give him fifty slaves. Especially considering her father didn't want her to marry Leo.

Leo was insane.

Zwaantie turned from him and raced to her room. Last night was long, and she needed to rest. And she wanted to forget about her horrible morning. She threw herself down onto her bed and dissolved into tears. Luna sat next to her and rubbed her back, speaking

Luna spoke quietly. "I know you were planning on exchanging your wedding for the release of slaves, but I didn't know you were going for fifty. That was extravagant. Don't you think?"

"I wanted exactly three. The prince is the one who decided we needed fifty."

"Three?"

"Yes, you, Phoenix, and Pieter."

Luna didn't respond, but Zwaantie felt her stiffen. Then Luna leaned across and hugged her shoulders. It wasn't much, but Zwaantie knew Luna was grateful for what she asked for.

That evening, just as Zwaantie was dressing for dinner, Leo came barging into her room. He didn't even knock. He had a huge smile on his face as he swooped her up in a hug and kissed her on the lips.

She didn't respond at first, but then returned the kiss. She didn't want him to be suspicious. Their lips moved easily against each other. It was nice, but there was no fire. No spark.

She pulled away as the Voice berated her. *Filthy slut. Remove yourself at once.*

She gave Leo a fake grin. "I'm sorry, but it's the Voice. It doesn't think we should kiss."

Leo frowned. "But we're engaged. Surely we're allowed to kiss when we're engaged."

"Chaste kisses only. Also, we aren't actually engaged. Father said no."

The pain in her head dissipated.

"Ah, but we have an agreement. Fifty slaves will come with us. My choice."

Zwaantie beamed at him. "I didn't think you could do it."

"Well, I hope you have more faith in me in the future. Are you ready for dinner?"

"Not quite, Luna has to braid my hair."

Leo sprawled out on the couch across from the

chair where Luna waited to do her hair.

Leo looked at her. "You know, she did this for you. Besides your husband and brother is there anyone else you'd like to bring with?"

She shook her head. "I've already spoken to Mother. She doesn't want to leave." Zwaantie was relieved by this. She'd have no trouble getting Luna. But the rest of her friends might be more difficult to release. She might get away with Pieter, but asking for the queen's slave as well would be too much.

"Can you do me a favor and find families who want to leave? I don't want to separate any of them. I won't get to choose until Sunday morning when we leave. But here." He handed her a small bag. "The bag contains fifty coins from Stella. Give them to the people who are to come with. Then when the king announces that he is ready for me to choose, I will ask for those coins back. That is how I will know who is coming."

Luna smiled at Zwaantie. "This is a smart one you've got here."

It worried her. If he was so smart, then how was she going to escape? He'd see right through her plan. Leo looked her over.

"Why do you insist on wearing such awful clothes?" Leo asked.

Zwaantie glared at him. "Rude, much?"

"You cover up everything. There is no room for creativity and fun. I brought you a trunkful of dresses. Why don't you wear one of them?"

"Because they are hideous. Not a single one would cover up what needs to be covered."

That's right. Good girl. That was odd. The Voice never complimented her before.

"You mean like your breasts? They are meant to be shown off a little." His eyes twinkled, and Zwaantie knew he was teasing her, but her breasts had always made her self-conscious.

Zwaantie sat down across from him. Teasing could go both ways.

"And why were you looking at my breasts?"

"Why not? Seriously, I just want to see cleavage. I suppose I could just wait until our wedding night, but where's the fun in that? Besides, I made a bet with Hunter, and I want to win."

Hunter grimaced in the corner.

Zwaantie narrowed her eyes at Leo. "What bet?"

Leo ignored her, opened the trunk, and pulled out a shimmery purple and green dress that had no sleeves and would probably show off her underwear if she bent over.

"Why don't you wear this one to dinner?"

"Not on your life."

"Why?"

"Because my mother would kill me. And my father might kill you. We don't wear clothes like that in Sol."

"What is it with you people and rules? Haven't you ever broken one?"

Zwaantie sighed. "Yes, of course I've broken rules. Who hasn't?"

"Then break this one. Wear the dress. Please."

"No."

He sighed, defeated, and sauntered over to Hunter. "I guess you were right. She never has disobeyed mommy." Leo handed him a few coins.

"What the dark?" Zwaantie asked.

"Hunter said you wouldn't do it because you never broke rules. I disagreed. But he won. What a boring wife you are going to be." He raised his eyebrows in a challenge.

"And what an arrogant cow-hole you are going to be. Why did I ever agree to marry you?"

"I've been asking myself that same question since you came to my room this morning. You obviously dislike me, and you have no interest in Stella, so why?"

Oh, he was smart. There was no way she would get away from him easily when they got to Stella. This would take more planning than she thought.

"You wouldn't understand. But I'm not changing my mind."

She stalked out of her room and went to dinner. Leo chatted with Father and Mother, and no one seemed upset by the arrangements that had been made. Hunter sat next to Zwaantie.

"Don't let him get to you. He's just trying to figure out your true motives."

"What?" Now she was nervous.

"He knows you don't love him. But what he doesn't know is why you want to marry him. Don't get me wrong, he's totally okay with marriage for other motives. He's completely smitten, and he was going to marry you no matter what."

Zwaantie sputtered for a second. "What do you mean he's completely smitten? He barely knows me."

"Oh, I've told him the same thing, but he was lost the second he laid eyes on you. I've never seen him look at someone like that before, and we've been friends for a long time."

Zwaantie let out a breath. She wasn't prepared for something like that. She didn't want to think that she'd actually hurt him. It was one thing to leave him if she thought he was just doing this to join their kingdoms. It was quite another if he was in love with her. She'd never love him though. Not the way she loved Phoenix.

"Do me a favor," Hunter said.

"Maybe." Zwaantie wasn't going to commit to

anything.

"Just don't break his heart. I don't care what your motives are, but he loves you."

She nodded, not daring to lie out loud. She was disgusted with herself.

Luna wasn't feeling good during dinner, so Zwaantie sent her home. Zwaantie worried about her. She hoped she wasn't coming down with something bad.

After dinner, Leo walked Zwaantie to her room, and Hunter miraculously disappeared. She'd never seen Leo without him. He followed her into her room, as if that was okay.

He sprawled out on her bed and looked at Zwaantie expectantly.

"It will be gray soon," she said. She didn't want him in her room after midnight. Who knew what would happen. Nothing good, that's for sure. Phoenix had been a gentleman. Leo was not.

"We have time," he said drowsily. "Come here."

Don't listen to him. Get him out of your room.

She sat tentatively on the edge of the bed, and pain flashed across her forehead.

You are playing with danger.

"Would you relax?" he asked.

"You are in my room with me alone and are on my bed. Not exactly relaxing for me." Especially with the

Voice reminding her how dangerous it was.

"I'm have no intention of taking advantage of you tonight. I just want to talk. And those chairs of yours are bloody uncomfortable. I won't even touch you, but lay here with me and talk. And take that stupid dress off."

"I thought you said you weren't going to do anything to me, yet here you are trying to get me to take my clothes off."

She gave him a smile to show she was joking and felt instantly guilty. She shouldn't enjoy her time with him. He was a road to Phoenix. That was all.

"Put something else on then. Something comfortable."

Zwaantie escaped behind her dressing screen. But try as she might, she couldn't get the laces on the back of her dress undone.

"Leo, can you help me?"

He nearly fell out of the bed trying to get to her. Probably thought she had less on.

"I can't get the laces. Can you?"

He undid the laces, lingering at the bottom of her spine. His fingers were soft and gentle. "Anything else?" he asked, his voice gruff.

"No, I think I got it."

Zwaantie put on a nightgown, which was just as modest as her dress but more comfortable. She lay down on the edge of her bed. Far enough away that he couldn't touch her, but close enough to talk.

"What do the stars look like?" she asked.

He smiled, and it was a nice smile. "Millions of tiny lights scattered across the navy blue sky. I miss them. It's so bright here all the time. The stars are harder to see in the cities, but out on the ocean you can see them all."

"I think that is what I am most looking forward to. Seeing the stars. Isn't it scary in the dark?"

He laughed. "It's never completely dark in Stella. I mean, we have no sun, but that doesn't mean we have a shortage of light. Sometimes it's brighter there than here. But our lights are different colors."

"How?" Zwaantie asked. The idea of brightness in Stella surprised her.

"Magic. I'll show you sometime how they do it. It's pretty amazing."

They talked for a while about Stella and all the things he would show her.

The midnight hour comes. Get him out.

"It's nearly midnight. You should go."

He sighed. "Why?"

"Because you can't be in here after midnight. We might do something we'd regret."

"We are going to be married. How much could we regret?"

Zwaantie shook her head. "You need to go. Now."

He sat up. "Okay, I'll go, but under one condition."

"And what's that?"

"On Saturday night, the night of the dance, I want you to wear one of the dresses I brought you."

Zwaantie almost argued with him, but midnight was approaching quickly.

"Okay. I'll wear one. But I get to pick."

"Excellent."

He kissed her on the lips and disappeared. The Voice didn't say anything. It must've been chaste enough.

She waited for about ten minutes and then heard her lock click. Locked in for the night.

The Voice in her head cleared with the midnight hour, and she wondered why she didn't want to wear the dresses. She pulled out the trunk and opened it. Each dress was had more than one color. She didn't realize that dresses could be that beautiful. In Sol, the clothes only contained one solid color. They may have adornments and things, but the color was always solid.

The first dress she pulled out was a red dress with no sleeves that had a long black ruffled train. She jerked off her nightgown and pulled the dress on. It fit perfectly. Almost too small and it pushed her breasts up. The dress made her feel alive.

She twirled around and giggled. Then she stripped it off and tried on another. Before collapsing into bed, she tried on all of the dresses and picked the one she would wear to the dance.

The dress was a deep black dress with bright blue jewels. It was the dress Mother would hate the worst. No sleeves and way, way too short.

Chapter 26

The Dance

The evening of the dance, butterflies fluttered in Zwaantie's belly. She and Luna had spent most of the day packing Zwaantie's things because they would leave for Stella in the morning.

Zwaantie pulled out the dress. The material flowed through her fingers.

"That's a little short. And revealing. Are you sure your mother will be okay with that?" Luna asked with raised eyebrows.

"I'm not wearing it for her."

Filthy. You know better. Put the dress back in the trunk and put on one of your own dresses. NOW.

The dress fit well. Zwaantie gave Luna the shoes she had found in the trunk. They had high heels and tiny blue jewels on the toes. They pinched her toes.

Slut. That's what you are. Take the dress off and put on something decent.

A small headache appeared behind her eyes. She didn't want to be in pain the whole evening, but she wanted to wear this dress.

Zwaantie tried to push the thoughts away. Guilt

gnawed at her insides, and her headache grew. On her bedside table sat the necklace Leo had presented to her when he arrived. She'd never worn it, thinking it was stupid to need protection because the Voice kept everyone from committing crimes.

Now though, she needed it. Someone was trying to kill her. She wished she'd thought of this earlier. She put it on, and her headache disappeared. A knock sounded at the door, and Luna answered it.

"I don't think this is a good time. Zwaantie is getting ready."

"I don't care. I need to talk to my sister before she leaves." Raaf pushed his way into the room, followed by his new slave. Zwaantie's heart clenched at the site of him. It should've been Phoenix.

"What are you wearing?" Raaf asked and quickly averted his eyes. His slave wasn't quite as discreet. His mouth dropped open. Zwaantie gave him a wink.

"A dress. From Stella. Why don't you sit?"

Raaf shook his head, still not looking directly at her. "Mother is not going to let you wear that."

"By the time Mother sees the dress, it will be too late. What did you want to talk about? We have a dance to attend."

Raaf sat, meeting her eyes. He creased his eyebrows and pulled her hands into his own. He'd never been so affectionate before. "Are you going to be okay in Stella? I can get you out of this marriage if you want. You don't seem happy with Leo."

Zwaantie gave him a sad smile. If he only knew. "Of course this is what I want. When have I ever done anything that I haven't wanted to?"

"I know. But I just want to make sure you'll be okay. Do you need anything from me? We probably won't get to talk much before you leave."

Zwaantie hugged him. "I'll miss you too, baby brother, but I'll be fine. Besides, it's only for a year. Then I'll be queen. That's a scary thought."

He grimaced. "Yeah, it is. Can I escort you to the dance? I won't be able to do that after you are married."

She almost invited him to come with on the tour of Stella, but then remembered that she wouldn't be coming back because she and Phoenix would run away once he had his bands removed. And that made her sad.

Zwaantie entered the grand hall, and her breath caught in her throat. Normally, banners of the sun and bright colors covered the room, but today half of the banners had been replaced with stars and a moon. They stood out in such stark contrast to the bright sun. It was gorgeous.

"I can't believe you're joining Stella and Sol. This is historical," Raaf said.

Zwaantie didn't want to be historical. She wanted to be normal. But she'd do this for Phoenix. Even if they couldn't run away, she had to get him out of the sewers. She would marry Leo if that meant Phoenix could be free.

She searched for her parents. They stood on the opposite side of the hall deep in conversation with the lower king of Sonnenschein. Standing next to them was Leo. He wore light pants made of a shimmery silver material and no shirt. But he wore an open vest that matched her dress. His eyes met hers.

Zwaantie and Raaf approached their parents, and Leo slipped his arm around Zwaantie's waist and pulled her close to him.

"You look amazing," he whispered. "I take back everything I ever thought about you."

Zwaantie's mother turned and looked at her. Her face twisted into a combination of horror and revulsion. In a matter of seconds, Zwaantie could see a thousand different emotions cross her face.

Her mouth opened. Zwaantie was about to have it.

"What do you think of the dress my sisters sent for Zwaantie?" Leo said. "Doesn't she look gorgeous?"

Zwaantie's mother recovered and looked at Leo. Cleary, she'd forgotten he was there. Zwaantie could see her fingers trembling, but she was never one to be rude. “Of course, but I think perhaps she should find something to cover her shoulders.”

Leo didn’t respond but swept Zwaantie out onto the dance floor. He pulled her close and led her in a dance she was unfamiliar with. In Sol, they didn’t touch much when they danced and never like the embrace he had Zwaantie in. But between the choice of facing her mother and dancing close to Leo, Zwaantie chose Leo. Though she felt guilty for enjoying it. She should be thinking of Phoenix. Not Leo.

They danced all night long. Occasionally they would dance the traditional Sol dances, but mostly he held her, and she was bothered that she enjoyed his touch. She fit nicely in the prince’s arms. She noticed the Voice was silent. Strange, it never missed an opportunity to berate her.

That night he walked her to her room about eleven thirty. She was sorry to see the night end. She’d had a good time and found that she was altogether too comfortable with Leo. In another life, she’d marry him and be happy. But her heart belonged with Phoenix.

“I’m excited to bring you home. I think you’ll like Stella. And you’ll love Sage, my sister.”

He kissed Zwaantie again, long this time, and her

insides tickled. It was sweet, but she couldn't see herself marrying him. But she could see herself being his friend. Although after she betrayed him, she doubted he'd be interested in any kind of friendship.

Chapter 27

The Complication

Mother stood next to Zwaantie on the steps as several slaves packed the carriages. There were a few trunks with dresses and personal items, but most of what they brought was food.

Mother frowned at the slaves. "He's taking so many."

Zwaantie shrugged. "He felt I was worth it." She was studying all the slaves. She needed to find Phoenix. He had to be among them. There he was standing near the back, filthy but with a wide smile. His eyes were on her. She smiled back, her insides warming. She was so very close.

Mother followed Zwaantie's line of sight. She gasped and gripped Zwaantie's arm.

"Did you agree to marry the prince so you could get Phoenix? Do you think you'll just run away with him in Stella? Oh, I was such a fool. No wonder you wanted to marry a Stellan."

Zwaantie kept her face straight. She could not give anything away. "No. Mother, that won't be possible, but at least he won't be in the sewers anymore."

Mother pulled her close and whispered fiercely in her ear. "You better be telling the truth, because my reach is farther than you think. If you don't marry the prince, I will find you, and I will make sure Phoenix dies. And you will watch. Do you understand? You could start a war if you backpedal on this wedding. Why did you think we discouraged it from the beginning?"

"Is everything okay?" Leo asked, causing Zwaantie to jump.

Mother jerked back and gave Leo a sugary sweet smile. "Of course, dear. Zwaantie and I have never been apart. I'm going to miss her so much."

Zwaantie shook out of her mother's grasp and took a few steps down to meet Leo.

"Goodbye, Mother. We'll see you at the wedding."

Mother nodded but didn't say anything more.

"Are you sure you're okay?" Leo asked Zwaantie.

"I'm fine." Her heart raced, but she couldn't tell Leo why she was upset. She hoped she'd be able to get away from Leo before her Mother tried anything.

Luna approached with tears on her face.

"What's the matter?" Zwaantie asked.

"Why is Pieter not among the freed slaves?" Luna asked.

"I was not successful in obtaining the king's slave," Leo replied. "That's your husband, right? We do need to get going, or we'll never make it before midnight. Here, your midnight hours are relatively safe. In Stella, they are dangerous, so we must go?"

Zwaantie drew her best friend into a hug. "You can stay here. You don't have to go with me."

Luna gripped the back of Zwaantie's dress and held her close. Then she pulled away, wiping at her eyes.

"We prepared for this possibility. I'll come back to him after, well, after a while. I need to go with you."

"I'm sorry," Zwaantie whispered. "You should go say goodbye to him. Father won't begrudge you for that."

Chapter 28

The Betrayer

The horseless carriage was amazing. The seats were wide and comfortable. Soft music played from above Zwaantie's head, and the whole inside was lit in a silvery blue. Leo sat close and put his arm around her. She leaned into him feeling guilty for enjoying it. Again, she waited for the Voice, but it never came. Weird.

Hunter flung himself down on one of the wide seats. "I will be so glad to get home, where things are normal again. No offense, Zwaantie, but Sol is the most uncomfortable place I've ever been. Plus, I miss my wife. She's going to kill you, Leo."

He raised his eyebrows. "Why?"

"You told Candace this would only take a day or two. It's been a week. She's due any day now. If our baby was born while we dawdled here, she will be one unhappy mama."

Leo laughed. "I'm sure I can handle it. Candace has been mad at me before. I thought our timing was pretty swift actually."

Hunter grunted. "Whatever."

Hunter was not a slave, but the way he talked to Leo, it was like he was his friend, his equal. Luna was curt with her sometimes, but they'd been friends before, so Zwaantie allowed it. It gotten worse since Phoenix, but then Luna was his sister. Phoenix. He would be free in less than twelve hours, and then they could get married. The excitement was almost too much for her.

She was excited for more reasons than one. When she and Phoenix ran away, she'd have something she'd never had before. Freedom. No responsibility. No nagging that she was doing something dishonorable.

The wall came into view, black and ominous. They rode along the road next to the wall for about thirty minutes. Then they stopped abruptly.

"They'll need to hook the carriages to the chains and give instructions to those who are walking how to get across the wall," Leo said, climbing out of the carriage. Zwaantie and the rest followed.

She peered around him to the waiting slaves. "How will they get across?"

"They'll hold to the Rod of Lost Memories. It spans the width of the wall. As long as they don't let go, they'll be fine. But there's more to crossing the wall than just walking across it."

"What do you mean?"

"The wall demands payment. It will take a memory. Whatever you are thinking about when you cross the wall is a memory you will no longer have on the other side."

"So if I think of something bad, I won't have to remember it anymore?"

"Exactly. But it's best to do something unimportant. Bad memories usually have too many other things attached them that don't make sense if you lose the memory. Choose carefully. You also will not remember anything that happens on the journey. It takes about a half hour by carriage. Two hours by walking."

Zwaantie tried to think of something. "And I won't remember the trip or what I was thinking of?"

"Nope. So make sure it is something you can live without. I need to go talk to Hunter. I'll be right back."

Zwaantie stared at the black mist. She crept around the carriage and stood as close as she dared to the wall. The tendrils whispered to her again, but she didn't have the Voice encouraging her to plunge into the wall's depths.

Zwaantie felt a hand on hers. She looked back and found herself face-to-face with Phoenix. They were alone, hidden behind the carriage. Her stomach buzzed.

"You did it," he said.

She beamed at him and placed a palm on his cheek. "I did. A few more hours, and this will be over."

He pulled her close, and she looked at him, surprised.

"Isn't the Voice telling you off?" she asked.

He whispered into her ear. "The Voice is strangely quiet. Maybe I'm too close to the wall."

That didn't seem right. The last time she was this close to the wall, the Voice was louder than ever. It was quiet now, but she suspected that had to do with the necklace Leo gave her.

She wanted to pull away and see if Phoenix had on a necklace as well, but he slid his hand up and around to the back of her neck. She shivered at the touch. He lightly stroked her jaw and tipped her chin so she could gaze into his gorgeous brown eyes.

"You're so beautiful," he said.

Zwaantie smiled. "Thank you."

He leaned down and brushed her lips with his own. Zwaantie reached her arms up and pulled him closer, deepening the kiss. Their lips moved furiously against one another. This was different from Leo. Her whole body was on fire. She pushed into him, wanting to be as close as possible. She'd been waiting for this moment since she first challenged him to that game of tag.

A voice came from behind her. "I can't believe this."

They sprang apart. Leo stood a few feet from her with a frown.

Zwaantie had no words. She had no way to explain. But if Leo refused to take them across the wall, her mother would kill Phoenix. Dammit. They couldn't wait a few more hours? What was she thinking?

Leo shook his head. "I understand now. You found out I could remove bondage bands. This was all some set up. You're going to run away with your slave lover when you get to Stella. I can't believe I was so stupid."

All the blood drained from her face. "This isn't what it looks like." He wouldn't fall for it. Of course, he wouldn't. But she had to try. She turned around to see if Phoenix could come up with some excuse, but he'd disappeared. What the dark?

Leo stalked closer to her. "Oh, don't play dumb, girl. I'm the spymaster of Stella. I can see all the clues. I can't believe I didn't see it before. I was too blinded by my own love."

"Oh, poor Zwaantie, all her plans falling apart."

Zwaantie turned around and found Wilma standing behind her.

"What are you doing here?" Zwaantie asked, thoroughly confused. Wilma wasn't supposed to be here. Not only that, but she was talking to Zwaantie like she was happy Zwaantie got caught.

Wilma tapped her fingers on her lips. "I came to say goodbye. Really, girl, I can't believe you are still alive."

"What do you mean?"

"You were smart, figuring out those connections," Wilma continued. "That silly slave girl was poisoned. That wine was meant for you."

Leo came to her side and stared at Wilma. Would he rescue her now? Or was he too angry? Zwaantie couldn't make sense of her words. "You were the one trying to kill me?"

"Oh, I most certainly wanted you dead, but no, dear. It wasn't me. It was the Voice. But you already know that."

She crept closer to Zwaantie, and Zwaantie backed up. The wisps of the wall slid across her shoulders.

Wilma leaned forward and whispered in her ear. "Before you die, I want you to know who it was that wanted you dead. You should die with the knowledge that someone you loved dearly was behind all those attempts. It will be I who succeeds, but still, you should know."

Zwaantie barely registered the name Wilma uttered. Instead, she spun and shoved Wilma right into the mist. Before she could back away though, Wilma's hand lashed out and pulled her right in.

Chapter 29

The Lost Memory

Leo didn't hesitate or even think. He plunged into the wall where Zwaantie disappeared. She could already be lost to the depths, but he had to try. Even if she had betrayed him.

He hit something solid and wrapped his arms around her waist. She struggled against his grip.

"Calm down, Zwaantie, it's me."

She stilled. "Leo."

He pressed his lips against her ear. "Yes, it's me. Where's the witch?"

"I don't know. She let go of me as soon as we fell. Why did you call her a witch?"

This was good. He wasn't sure where she went, but at least she wasn't with them.

"She's the Old Mother." He almost didn't recognize her. She looked different than she had when she visited, but those eyes were one of a kind.

Zwaantie's grip tightened. "How do you know of the Old Mother?"

"She's the reason I came over to Sol. But I'll explain that later. We need to get out of here."

Zwaantie pulled him back toward the way they fell in. “Thank goodness we aren’t far in.”

Leo chuckled. “Sorry, Princess, it doesn’t work like that. We’ll never get out if we try to go back.”

“Where are we going then?”

“Toward the Rod of Lost Memories. If we can find that, we’ll be able to get out okay. But we can’t waste any time. The longer we are in here, the more disoriented we’ll be.”

He pulled her toward the rod. He had an excellent sense of direction, and if he moved east, he’d hit the rod. If they didn’t find it, they’d be lost forever.

“Do you think Wilma will be able to get out?”

“Who?”

“The woman you called the Old Mother.”

“Probably. She’s the Old Mother after all. Why’d she want to kill you anyway?”

“I have no idea. She was my friend.”

Zwaantie went quiet, and Leo pressed through the darkness, his soon-to-be lost memory haunting him.

“Tell me, Princess, how long have you been planning to betray me?”

“You wouldn’t understand.”

“Try me. We have at least two hours in this mist, and we’re both going to forget this as soon as we step into Stella. You can at least do me the service of letting me know why.”

Zwaantie tugged her hand.

"Don't let go of me. You'll get lost."

"Why did you come after me anyway?"

"Because I love you. I have since the second I laid eyes on you. I've always thought my brothers and sisters were crazy when they talked about love at first sight, but now I understand. I can't explain it. I'd die for you."

She let out a sigh. "I'm sorry. I don't feel the same way. I wish I did. It would make this so much easier."

"Why did you agree to marry me?"

"You saw how Stella is about slaves. I saw an opportunity to free Phoenix. It was my only option. I didn't plan on falling in love with him, but it happened. Before I fell for him, I didn't even know love like that was possible. I can't imagine my life without him. I didn't mean to hurt you."

Leo almost stopped walking, but he couldn't. Intellectually, he understood what she was talking about. Love was something that grabbed ahold and didn't let go. He felt it for her. But the pain in his chest that she would do betray him like that was too much.

They had to keep pushing through the inky blackness.

His hip hit something solid. He reached down and found the steel rod. Thank the stars. They wouldn't perish. The two-inch rod floated at waist level. They could hold on tight and find their way home. Or back to Sol. He wasn't sure which way they'd go, but hopefully they'd exit in Stella.

He pulled Zwaantie over and placed her hand on the cool steel. "Hold onto this. If you let go, you'll disappear. We're lucky we found it. Stay close to me so I don't think I lost you."

"Okay."

They plodded on in silence for several minutes.

"You know, we won't remember anything of our conversations when we step out of the mist," he said.

Zwaantie snorted. "That means I can tell you anything, and you won't remember it."

"Exactly."

"So tell me something true. Something you didn't dare to tell me before," Zwaantie said.

The question surprised Leo. He didn't think she was terribly interested in his life. But since she was asking, he wanted her to understand what was at stake, even if she wouldn't remember on the other side. "If we don't get married, my sister's baby is going to die."

"Why?"

"The Old Mother. She gave a prophecy that said if Stella and Sol weren't joined by the first birthday of Candace's baby, then he would die, and he wouldn't be the last."

"That's awful. Why didn't you just tell me?"

Leo rolled his eyes. "You've got to be kidding me. The minute I walked into the castle, you accused me of having ulterior motives. Do you think you would have just agreed to marry me if you thought I was only doing it for my sister?"

"Probably not. But maybe we could've found another solution. Two minds are better than one. What would you have done if I hadn't agreed to marry you?"

"That's another secret. You're turn to tell me something true."

She was quiet for a few moments. "I don't want to be queen."

"Why not?"

"Because I'm not good at leading people, and I just want to live a normal life."

"Did you want that before you fell in love with Phoenix?"

"Yes. Maybe that's why I fell in love with him. He was my chance at normal. I never was the most obedient child, and I don't like the obligations that come with being queen. If you hadn't come along, Mother would've made me marry someone else who I didn't love. Phoenix or no Phoenix."

Leo didn't know what to think about that. He'd

never had to do anything he didn't want to. Sure, he wasn't crazy about going to Sol, but he did that because he loved his sister and wanted to help her, not because he had to.

In Stella, Zwaantie would have freedoms she couldn't even begin to imagine. She might run away with the slave. She might not. She wouldn't remember any of this when they stepped into his land, but stranger things had happened. Even if she did run away with her slave, they'd have a better life in Stella than they would in Sol. If she ran off, he'd have to return to his father, and they'd have to prepare for war.

Stella and Sol needed to be joined. He wouldn't let Candace's baby die.

They walked in silence for a while, both lost in their own thoughts. He wondered what memory she would forget. Probably her fight with the witch if that is what she was thinking about when she crossed the wall. She called the woman Wilma. For Zwaantie's sake, he hoped Wilma was lost in the mist because if not, Zwaantie would still trust her.

After another hour, he was going mad with the thoughts in his head. Thoughts that would disappear the second he stepped out of the mist.

"Tell me something else that you would never tell me if you thought I'd remember," Leo said.

"You're a good kisser."

Leo stopped dead, and she ran into him. That was not what he expected to come out of her mouth.

He spun around, let go of the steel rod, but kept his hip pressed against it. He wrapped his arms around her, pulled her against him. Stars, she felt good.

He leaned down so his face was close to her ear.

"But I thought you were in love with Phoenix."

She snaked her arms around his waist and held him close. He was completely taken aback. She laid her cheek against his chest.

"I am. But that doesn't mean you're a bad kisser. To be honest, if Phoenix had never been in the picture, we'd probably still be heading to Stella to plan the wedding. I like you. A lot more when the Voice isn't whispering in my head. I wish we could've been friends. I bet you would've helped me figure out how to run away with Phoenix."

He chuckled. "Probably. But at this point, even if Candace's baby wasn't in danger, I'm way too in love with you to help you run away with anyone else."

"I know," she mumbled.

He pulled away and found her face with his hands. "We're not far from the edge of the wall. When we step out of the darkness, we'll forget everything that happened in here. I'm going to forget that you are in love with Phoenix and will probably run away with him and betray me. You're going to be happy. But for just a few minutes, can you be mine?"

"Under one condition."

He felt her smile under his hands. "What's that?"

"Will you kiss me?"

His lips met hers, and for several minutes she was all his. He tried not to think about what was coming on the other side of the wall.

He took a step away from her.

"Thank you."

She didn't say anything, but took his hand in hers and squeezed. He kept one hand clasped in hers and one gripped on the rod. Ten feet later he stepped out of the blinding darkness and into the neon lights of Stella.

The End

I hoped you enjoyed reading God of The Sun. If you are interested in the next book in the series, Prince of the Moon, it will be released in April 2017 and can be pre-ordered here: www.kimberlyloth.com/prince

If you enjoyed this book, or even if you didn't, please consider leaving a review. As an Indie author, reviews are crucial.

Thank you for reading!

Check out this excerpt from Kimberly Loth's exciting series, *The Thorn Chronicles*.

Birthdays are supposed to be special like my Kaiser Wilhelm rosebushes. They bloom once a year, huge violet and crimson cups full to bursting with petals. When I part the petals with my nose and inhale, I go weak in the knees from the fruity perfume. But my birthdays are more like the daisies that grow alongside the roses. Ignored.

The sink looked odd next to our front door. My mother had it installed after I kept tracking in dirt and fertilizer from my greenhouse. I washed the soil off my hands with the warm water and used a file to clear the dirt out from under my nails. Then I exchanged one dirty pair of ugly tennis shoes for a pair of clean ugly tennis shoes and made my way into the kitchen. Mother didn't allow a speck of soil from my greenhouse to dirty her home.

Paint on the cabinets peeled away in white curls. A single light bulb gave enough light to cook but not enough to read a recipe. My mother stood by the tiny window, her bottle blond hair twisted in a bun on the back of her head. She wiped her hands on her apron then smoothed a stray hair from my braid. I knelt down to tie my shoes, anything to avoid her touch. Physical touch burned, even something as little as a finger brushing my forehead.

"Wash your face. We have guests for dinner." My stomach knotted. I tied and untied my shoes three times, wondering how to respond. Years ago, my father had closed our home to visitors. No one crossed our threshold. I was allowed to leave only to go to school and to church. Well, if you want to call it that. I've watched movies in school and I went to the Baptist church until I was eight. Our new church, Crusaders of God, was a bigger shock than no more pants. But Mother and Father called it church.

"Why?" I asked. My curiosity overrode my memory of the last question I asked when Grandma died and I wanted to know why I couldn't go to the funeral. I stood and waited for the slap and a lecture.

Instead, she smiled like she was hiding something important.

"For your birthday. They're friends of your father's from church. We have a big surprise for you."

Of course. Friends of my father. Nothing ever happened in our house unless he was the center of attention. Even on my birthday. At least they remembered. The surprise concerned me though, as the last surprise they announced turned out to be a drastic lifestyle change complete with long denim skirts and strict obedience. Oh, and no more birthdays. Until now, apparently. Maybe the surprise would be that my father finally found his sanity. That would be an amazing birthday present. I doubted I'd get that lucky.

Dinner took place in the dining room. The cheap chandelier struggled to fill the room with light as two of the bulbs were out and nobody bothered to replace them. Our mysterious dinner guest turned out to be familiar. And not the good kind of familiar either.

Dwayne Yerdin sat at the table. He was a senior at my school but ended up in quite a few of my classes even though he was two years older. I probably shouldn't judge him. But with his heavy lidded, half closed eyes, buzzed head, and classic bully laugh, I had disliked him the moment I saw him. Perhaps he would prove my judgment wrong tonight. Seated next to him was a pudgy man in a suit. He wore a tie, but his neck was too thick to fasten the top button. He had the same heavy lidded eyes as Dwayne.

My father, a tall thin man with thick blond hair, saw me waiting in the doorway.

"Naomi, it's about time. Come and meet Dwayne and his father. They go to church with us. Here, sit."

My father indicated the chair next to Dwayne, but

I sat across from him instead. My head buzzed with the act of disobedience and the air smelled faintly of wisteria. I almost smiled. A look of irritation passed over my father's face, but he didn't say anything. Next to my father, the pudgy man stared at me with piercing gray eyes.

My mother served us all pot roast and baked potatoes. She piled every plate high but hers and mine. Hunger kept me humble. And skinny. I focused on my food most of the dinner, not wanting to meet the pudgy man's gaze. Or Dwayne's. His eyes shifted rapidly around the room as if he were looking for the nearest exit. But when his eyes met mine he smirked, like he knew something I didn't.

My father and Mr. Yerdin talked of politics and religion, not once acknowledging that anyone else sat at the table. Of course, I shouldn't have been surprised since more than one sermon had been preached about the place of women and children. We were inferior and didn't deserve an opinion that differed from our husbands' or fathers', so it was best that we just didn't say anything at all. As the conversation turned to the medical experiments Dad performed on the dog that had been dumped in our yard last week, I tuned out and tried to think of what I would get if I crossed an Iceberg rose with a Sunsprite. A nice pale yellow and only a few thorns.

Could be interesting. If Grandma were still alive, she'd appreciate it.

A quick glance at the clock told me they'd only been here forty-five minutes, but it felt like days. After another excruciating hour, Mother presented the cake. The carrot cake (my father's favorite) had sixteen candles on it. I had not had a cake with candles since my eighth birthday. On that day, the cake was chocolate, my favorite, but that was before Father went insane. I missed those days, the ones before he went crazy. When he would come home and take me canoeing and fishing. When we would wake up early on Saturdays and go to breakfast at Sheila's Café. I blinked back tears thinking of the father he used to be.

After the cake, I moved to help my mother clean up, but Father put a hand on my wrist, a signal to stay seated. The skin burned where he touched it.

"See," my father said, "she's obedient."

Mr. Yerdin grinned. "Yes, of course she is. I wouldn't expect anything less from you, Dr. Aren. Dwayne, what do you think?"

Dwayne shrugged and shifted his eyes. Me, I kept my mouth shut and listened for the words that weren't being said.

Mr. Yerdin eyed me up and down. "Well, she certainly has the required blond hair and blue eyes."

"And she's a virgin." My father spoke this a little too loudly and I flinched. My mother paused before picking up Mr. Yerdin's plate. She met my father's eyes and nodded. Then the corners of her mouth turned up ever so slightly.

My stomach sank at the thought of what my birthday surprise would be. Although part of me did not want to hear the rest of the conversation, but to escape back into the quiet world of flowers and dirt, another part of me needed to know what my future held, where being a virgin was important.

I cleared my throat. Dwayne smiled a wide toothy smile and my father glowered like I'd done something wrong. Which, of course I had, but it would be worth the punishment if I got the answers I needed.

"Could someone please explain?" There. I asked the question. So out of character for me and yet satisfying in a strange way, like the way I felt when a teacher praised me for a good job. I bit my bottom lip and tasted butterscotch, which was weird because the cake we had, contained nothing of the sort. While I knew asking questions was not an act of disobedience, I also recognized the power in the asking. As if I was taking control, even if that control was small. I took a sip of my water. Father hesitated for a moment and then frowned. He looked up and saw my mother standing in the kitchen, her eyes boring into his. He didn't look away from her when he answered me.

"You'll be marrying Dwayne."

About The Author

Kimberly Loth can't decide where she wants to settle down. She's lived in Michigan, Illinois, Missouri, Utah, California, Oregon, and South Carolina. She finally decided to make the leap and leave the U.S. behind for a few years. She spent two wild years in Cairo, Egypt. Currently, she lives in Shenzhen, China with her husband and two kids as a full time author. She loves romantic movies, chocolate, roses, and crazy adventures. She's the author of Amazon bestselling series *The Dragon Kings.*

Also by Kimberly Loth

The Thorn Chronicles
Kissed: www.kimberlyloth.com/kissed
Destroyed: www.kimberlyloth.com/destroyed
Secrets: www.kimberlyloth.com/secrets
Lies: www.kimberlyloth.com/lies

The Dragon Kings
Obsidian: www.kimberlyloth.com/obsidian
Aspen: www.kimberlyloth.com/aspen

Valentine: www.kimberlyloth.com/valentine
Skye www.kimberlyloth.com/skye
The Kings www.kimberlyloth.com/kings

Omega Mu Alpha Brothers
Snowfall and Secrets: www.kimberlyloth.com/snowfall
Pyramids and Promises:
www.kimberlyloth.com/pyramids
Folly and Forever: www.kimberlyloth.com/folly
Monkeys and Mayhem:
www.kimberlyloth.com/monkeys

Stella and Sol
God of the Sun: www.kimberlyloth.com/sun
Prince of the Moon (April 2017):
www.kimberlyloth.com/moon
King of the Stars (May 2017):
www.kimberlyloth.com/stars
Queen of the Dawn (June 2017):
www.kimberlyloth.com/monkeys

Acknowledgements

I have the most amazing editors. Suzi and Kelley, thank you so much for all the hard work you put into helping me craft my novels. (And answering my thousands of questions.)

Milo, I know we had a few words about the cover, but it's beautiful. Thank you.

Jaye, I'm so glad I found you! Thank you for helping make my books beautiful.

Brittany, once again, your proofreading skills are superb. Thank you.

Peachy, thanks so much for beta reading for me and making sure I get out of the house once in a while for good food.

Also, a special thank you to Cherry, Tiffany, Virginia, and my kiddos for catching those typos.

Virginia, could I ever thank you enough? I don't think so. THANK YOU THANK YOU THANK YOU THANK YOU THANK YOU THANK YOU THANK YOU THANK YOU THANK YOU THANK YOU THANK YOU THANK YOU THANK YOU THANK YOU THANK YOU THANK YOU THANK YOU THANK YOU THANK YOU...

I have the most amazing family. When I started writing they were all so supportive. Not just my husband, kids, and mom either. Cousins. Aunts. Even second in law cousins once removed (looking at you Ben). I'm so, so grateful for all of your support. Thank you.

My husband is a patient man. He's waited four long years for me to dedicate a book to him. You see this story came to me rather quickly several years ago. I wrote a quick 30,000 word draft, but I felt like it was a little too big for me. So I shelved it, but not before reading the first draft to him. He told me that it was the best book I've ever written. Since then, anytime anyone asks him about my books, he always says, "Just wait, that's not even the good one." So here you go baby, the good one. Thanks for being my most ardent supporter. Love you.

My superfans. I love you. Thank you for your amazing support. A huge shout out to Amanda Showalter, Amber Christiansen, Andrea Hubler, Angie Blankenship, Anne Loshuk, Ashley Martinez, Belinda Tran, Brianna Snowball, Caitlin Simmons, Cassandra Sue Dahlin, Chris Radentz, Dawn Foster, Denise Austin, Diane Norwood, Donna Wolz, Emily Pennington, Ginger Calkins, Hanife Ormerod, Isis Ray-Sisco,, Jai Henson, Jennifer LaRocca, Jennifer Jeray, Jennifer McIntosh, Katheline V. Wziontko,

Katie Odom, Kaylee Truax, Laurie Murray, Linda Levine, Lyn Mckenzie, Mary Hazelwood, Mary Martin, Michelle McLain, Nikki Christensen, Patti Hays, Patty Bercaw, Samantha Endy, Samantha Murphy, Sara Groenheide, Sarah Jonak, Sarah Moon, Seraphia "Bunny" Sparks, Shelly Ash, Stephanie Pittser, Suzanne Hager-Cobb, Tera Comer, and Zoe Gregory. Thank you so much!!!

CPSIA information can be obtained
at www.ICGtesting.com
Printed in the USA
FSOW01n2311040118
43083FS